Crime of Silence

ALSO AVAILABLE BY PATRICIA CARLON

The Souvenir
The Whispering Wall
The Running Woman
The Price of an Orphan

Crime of Silence

Patricia Carlon

First published in Great Britain by Hodder and Stoughton

Copyright © 1965 by Patricia Carlon; first published in the
United States of America in 1998

Published by
Soho Press, Inc.
853 Broadway
New York, NY 10003`

Library of Congress Cataloging-in-Publication Data
  Carlon, Patricia, 1927–
        Crime of silence / Patricia Carlon.
            p.   cm.
        ISBN 1-56947-172-X (alk. paper)
        I. Title.
    PR9619.3.C37C7   1998
    823—dc21   98-15803
                                    CIP

10 9 8 7 6 5 4 3 2 1

CHAPTER ONE

WINTON said, "Kiley? I don't remember . . ." then as the staccato speech cut across his own words his body tightened, his voice growing crisper and colder as he broke in himself. "The *Galaxy*? I don't give interviews to the press." Then, as his gaze went to the grey square of window where the venetians had been rolled up, surprise wiped out the coldness. "Especially at . . . what is it?" he half twisted so he could see the clock, "at half past six in the morning. Are you crazy?"

The staccato speech was louder, as though trying to batter him into silence. He listened for a moment, then said, surprise and anger both gone, "I don't discuss my daughter with anyone. I've nothing . . ."

The other voice drowned his, in anger this time, and in pleading. Winton went on listening for a long time. Then he said slowly, but there was lingering doubt in his voice, "I guess you can come on out," and put the receiver down. He stood there for a long moment, gently rubbing the ball of one bare foot over the toes of the other, then he reached across the table for cigarettes.

Lighting one, he stood smoking for exactly five minutes, his gaze on the gilt hands and figures of the clock, then he crushed out the cigarette, reaching for the phone again, dialling quickly.

He said, "Jack? Can you remember an article in the *Galaxy* about someone called Evan Kiley? And some land? And a new bridge? And a highway? Give me what you can remember."

He listened in silence, till finally he said slowly, "Thanks. No, I can't tell you yet if I want it followed up. Leave it for the moment and I'll let you know."

He padded softly out of the room, a short, slight man whose narrow shoulders were swamped in the crumpled folds of green and white cotton pyjamas.

The bungalow was quiet with the early hush of morning and when he padded on to the thick blue carpeting of the big bedroom jutting from the side of the long, low building, Annie was still in the same position, white shoulders bare above the rim of sheet and her long hair a flame of red across the pillow.

He said almost diffidently, on a rising note of gentle enquiry, "Annie?"

She mumbled something against the pillow and one plump arm moved slightly, but when he spoke her name again she rolled over, the dark blue of her eyes still filmed with sleep. He watched the dawn of awareness come into them, then she said, without rancour, "Beast."

"We'll have visitors in one hour. Seven-thirty." He sat down on his own side of the rumpled bed.

"Beast," she repeated and reached out. She murmured, arms round him, one flushed cheek rubbing softly across his lips, "Love of a beast . . ."

"No." He reached up and unclasped her fingers. Still holding them, but sitting up again, he said quietly, "We're going to talk about Victoria's going . . ."

She had made a murmur of protest, given an impatient movement at his first word, then she became quite still.

He went on, "This man—his name's Kiley—wants to talk about it."

"Why?"

"Because his son has gone. So he says."

The sick shock that had started into her face died out as she repeated, "So he *says*. Don't you . . . ?"

"I didn't know whether to believe him or not. It could be a trick. He's a newspaper man, but he told me some details about himself and I rang Jack Haines—he filled

6

me in. Kiley owns some land that's become valuable—worth sixty thousand. The press has spread the story. That's fact, Annie. Still . . . I don't know. But you'd maybe better get up."

"Oh my god!" It didn't sound like simple swearing. It sounded to him like a prayer. Like a beaten soul who had rejoiced in peace, only to find the beating renewed. He knew how she felt and he couldn't help her. That was the worst of it.

He said, trying to bring her out of the pain of memory, "Annie, my Annette . . ." and was instantly lost in memory himself, thinking of the first time he had seen her, when he had cried, "Annette? *Annette* O'Brien? Who landed you with that?"

She had wrinkled her nose and laughed at him, "My mum. The poor dear was a romantic, but my dad says I'm'n Irish Annie right enough."

But even his voice wasn't capable then of reminding her of the meeting and their laughter. He knew, as he left her and stepped under the shower, that all she could think of —all she would think of till Kiley had told his tale, and maybe all she would be able to think of for ages after was half of a week eight months before. She'd remember nothing else, not their first meeting or the long way they had both come since then—himself from behind a hotel desk to owner of a chain of motels, and Annie from a grocery in the near slums to a well-to-do matron in a luxury home on the Gold Coast.

He towelled himself dry and opened the window, so that the drumming of the tropical downpour sounded louder still and a glitter of raindrops splashed through the wet gold of the fly screen on to the white painted windowsill. He sniffed vigorously at the sodden, clear air after the muggy warmth of the closed house and then noticed that one of the big black spiders that lurked among the garden

7

foliage had come through a ventilator and was sprawled in ungainly hideousness against the white of the bath, like a disgusting stain. He was reminded of the hideousness that had stained his and Annie's lives eight months before and in sudden fury he turned on both taps, sending a cascade of surging water gurgling into the bath to catch the spider and swirl it, struggling in frantic movements, down the plug hole to oblivion.

Before he went downstairs he looked into the nursery, but three-year-old Victoria was still asleep. She looked, even with her babyish roundness of feature, a complete miniature of Annie, he reflected, and was suddenly gazing into the future, seeing her coming downstairs one day, not to his own arms, but to another man's. Like Annie she would always look her best in evening dress, with her wide, cream-coloured shoulders bare, and a skirl of skirt swirling round small coloured slippers. He felt a sudden surge of resentment towards the unknown man who would on that future day wait her coming, with stars in her eyes for him. He gave a sudden low-toned chuckle, touched the hump that was her two small feet and went out of the room, carefully closing the door behind him.

When he went out Annie was already in the sun-room, wearing a straight blue linen shift and thong sandals, her heavy red hair piled on top of her head. She said, "There's coffee in the kitchen, love." She was still seated there, gazing blankly ahead of her, when he came back with the filled cup. She asked, without looking up, "What did this chap tell you?"

"Just that his boy had gone and he's to be contacted to-day. He knows — I expect any pressman would — about the rumours."

Her head jerked round. She asked harshly, "Do you think this's a trick? To make us blab everything so they can spread it at last'n then . . ."

8

"We'll have to see, Annie. It could be. That's why I rang Jack. It's true enough Kiley's become well-off overnight, but . . . we'll just have to wait and judge, that's all."

She said, with a passionate intensity that held quivering pain, "It's got to be a trick, it's just got to be, because if it isn't . . ." then she fell silent again.

He was lost in memory and knew she was, too. Memory of endless nights of warm darkness; of padding to and fro between their room and the nursery "just to make sure she's all right" just once more. Over and over again. And in between the endless whispering debate of whether to tell or not; whether to speak out or remain silent and perhaps have it happen to someone else, sometime, somewhere, in the future ahead, and know part of the blame could be laid at their own doorstep.

Endless debates, endless whispering, endless decisions made and rescinded and made again, all boiling down in the end to silence.

And now? If the unknown man of the phone was to be believed he and Annie could have become criminals by their silence, as surely as if they had committed some crime with their own hands against Kiley's child. He knew that if it was proved instead to be a trick that his own relief would be so great he would probably let Kiley go without a word.

When the bell rang he went out into the hall without looking at Annie, but knowing she was following after him. Mrs. Gage, the housekeeper, was coming, heavy-footed, from the kitchen and he waved her back. He opened the door and the gale wind came rushing in, tugging at his clothes as it tugged at the clothes of the pair on the doorstep. He stood aside to let them come in, while he silently surveyed them—the man much taller than himself—six feet, Winton judged, and perhaps eight or ten years younger than his own forty-two, thickset and brown

9

haired, with pale shadowed eyes in a long freckled face; the woman small and fine-boned, grey eyed, with a tangle of long dark hair windspun round her pointed face. She pressed against the pearl grey of the wall behind her as though tiredness was taking over her body. He saw Annie move, going closer to the other woman, and noticed how frail the stranger looked beside Annie's vibrant big body.

Then he said huskily, "You're Evan Kiley," and nodded to the woman. "Your wife?"

"Yes." The man's voice was low, holding a note of reserve, sounding far different to the clipped, staccato of the speech over the phone. "Miriam. Miram Stead, as she prefers to be known."

And why does she prefer that, Winton wondered, but the thought was pushed aside in the pressing need to know whether Kiley's story was a trick, or worse. He asked, "Your son's gone?"

"Yes." Then in sudden challenge, letting his pale gaze hold the older man's, he said, "You don't trust me, do you? Because I'm a pressman. But it's true. My boy's gone. He's fifteen months old and has fair hair and grey eyes and a dimple in his chin and he's wearing a white sleeping suit with a crazy blue pony embroidered on the front of it, and I don't know where he is. He's fat and a bit bow-legged and he's allergic to cow's milk. Do you think whoever's got him will know that? Or will they . . ."

He broke off. His pale eyes held a strangely shining appearance. He said, "I'm sorry. But if you'll only listen . . ."

CHAPTER TWO

WHEN Kiley started to speak his voice was low and rapid, as though all the events were being lived there again in front of his eyes.

The smell of gas, he said, was his first awareness when he opened the door. He stood there in the small hallway, lifting his head, sniffing, connecting the smell with the fact that the house was in complete darkness when it shouldn't have been. There should have been faint light from the nursery where fifteen-month-old Robin slept, and brighter light from at least one of the other rooms, where Irene would be waiting his return home. He remembered how he had slid the grey Holden to a halt, with the sea dark on his right and the bald-crowned hill that gave Comboroo its name, dark on his left, and had sat there smoking, quite unconscious of any selfishness, only of the satisfied acceptance that however late he returned, Irene Suttle would still be in the house with Robin.

The smell of gas catching at thought again, he called tentatively, "Irene!" and heard his voice echo, without receiving an answer. He thought suddenly that of course there must be a gas leak somewhere and Irene had taken the boy and gone to her own home next door. Because his mind was used to connecting a story to pictures, he had a sudden mental vision of Irene, with Robin's plump, heavy body caught close to her own thin figure, hurrying through the rain with the cold storm wind whipping at her blonde hair.

He half turned, on the heels of the thought and mental picture, going back to the white front step and standing there to look across the low dividing fence towards the other house.

The mental picture had been so vivid he stared blankly at the darkened house for a full half minute before the awareness of the smell touched him again. Then he turned, calling sharply, "Irene!" and went hurrying in, switching on lights in the hallway, in the small front room he used as a home office, and in the lounge with its one wall of glass looking out towards the sea.

His hand was still on the double switch there when the telephone rang. His reaction was automatic, the response of a man long accustomed to the telephone ruling both nights and days with its possible lead to a story that would make the next day's headlines.

The smell of gas, even the thought of Irene and Robin, were suddenly thrust into the background of consciousness as he lifted the receiver and said crisply, "Evan Kiley speaking."

There was a silence so long that the smell of gas and the anxiety for Irene and the boy came surging back, so that he cried in irritation, "Evan Kiley here. Who is it?"

"Don't be a fool and summon the police," the voice told him. "We have your son. We'll ring again at noon tomorrow. Don't be a fool and go running to the police."

It took him a long moment of slow, careful movement before he had the receiver away from his ear and replaced in its cradle. He had a queer light-headed, throat-catching feeling as he moved quietly, a quietness that was at variance with his thickset build, to the right of the hallway. His hand closed round the flower-painted porcelain doorknob of the room beyond the bathroom, and pushed inwards. He stood there listening for the soft sound of breathing, while nerves began to prickle. There was always a faint light in the nursery. The boy wouldn't sleep without it. Now it was out and he was remembering how the phone had rung just the instant the house lights had gone on, as though they had served the purpose of telling someone out in the storm-ridden night that he had returned home.

His hand flicked out and down on the light switch and he was looking at the cot, cream-painted, with a yellow duck in a necklace of pink and blue flowers tossed into the foot of it among the blue blankets and white sheets.

There was no sign of Robin. When he crossed to the cot and put his hand flat on the sheets they felt cold. As though the boy had been gone a long, long time.

Looking down at his hand he saw with vague detachment that the thin fingers, so much at variance, again, with his thick-set five feet eleven, were faintly trembling. He lifted them away from the cold sheet, but went on staring down at the empty cot. The only thing he could think or feel was the absurd wonder that someone, some stranger, could have lifted the child and taken him away without Robin stirring from his usual light sleep and roaring the place down—without Irene rushing to see what was wrong.

And where *was* Irene anyway? He lifted his gaze from the cot in sudden shock. Movement came flowing back into him. As he went out of the nursery he was telling himself in rising anger that it was a fool trick; that Irene had taken the boy away for some reason; because of the leak of gas he thought in sudden thankfulness. She hadn't been able to find the gas-cock to turn it off. She had probably put Robin in his pushchair and taken him to neighbours, and someone had seen her go and called up . . . frightening him. He'd made plenty of enemies in his journalistic career—he could name half a dozen round Comboroo who hated his guts for the stories he'd printed about them and their activities.

He thrust open the closed kitchen door and was beaten backwards by the outpouring of gas that flowed to meet him, together with a queer, rancid smell of burning. Walking backwards, he kept thrusting open doors and windows, till the drapes over the glass wall of the lounge were rustling in their golden taffeta folds with a sound like the angry murmur of disturbed bees, and he could smell the bitter-sweet smell of rain drenched earth come flowing in above the smell of gas.

He wet a towel in the bathroom, holding it over mouth and nose as he went back into the kitchen, to see what he had half expected. One of the burners of the gas range was full on, but the flame was out. There was a sticky mess of something all down the sides of a saucepan and over the burner beneath it. He slammed down the tap, managing to thrust the window wide in the room before running out again.

He stood in the hallway again and for the first time really dwelt on the thought that the soft voice had been talking sense—that someone had actually taken Robin away.

That someone had been in the house—some alien person —was definite. Robin was gone and so was Irene. The lights had been switched off, so that their being relit would signal his return to someone who had watched from outside. Irene must have been warming something—soup, cocoa, he didn't know what—when she was disturbed. By what? By someone coming in? By the boy crying? By the telephone ringing? She had hurried away and the saucepan's contents had boiled over, putting out the flame, and she hadn't been able to come back and turn off the gas.

His hand groped for cigarettes, then slid away as he remembered that a flame then might cause an explosion. He went on standing there, still smelling the gas, wondering if Irene was with the boy; if he was crying; or if perhaps Irene had been lured out of the house by a telephone call. He couldn't imagine what might have been said to her. He could imagine even less her going and leaving the boy quite alone, though if she had expected him back very shortly she might have taken the risk. But she would have left a note, he thought suddenly. Surely she would have done that.

He went back into the big lounge room, searching, and then into the room he used as an office, with its green filing cabinets of clippings and its battered desk, but there was nothing there either.

It was then he thought of Miriam and blinding rage took over from groping thought. He was back in memory to the night six months before when he and Miriam had had their last violent quarrel and she had flung out of the house. He remembered his own threats then and her counterthreats and his retorts. It had been a volcanic explosion throwing out into the open all the hatred and bitterness of their marriage. Miriam had been deaf to reason then. She had set her heart on returning to the stage which she'd left on her marriage. As he had pointed out, over and over again, she had left it willingly enough. "But I never intended to leave it for ever," she had protested, a protest that had changed to bitterness and bitterness that had changed to anger and then to hatred as he had dug in his heels and refused to leave Comboroo for the city so she could have both her marriage and the career she wanted.

He had expected her to quieten down with Robin's coming, but afterwards he had realized that the enforced inactivity of the months of waiting, when the doctors had told her she had to rest or suffer serious consequences, had only activated the restlessness and bitterness that had finished in their flaming row when Robin had been nine months old.

He remembered how he had told her that if she went she would have to leave Robin behind. He had expected that to clinch the argument, because with all her faults he thought she genuinely loved Robin. He remembered the

15

way she had thrown back her head and laughed and cried, "Can you see yourself? *You* of all people caring for a baby on your own? You'd have to get a housekeeper and she wouldn't and couldn't care for him the way I do."

He had pointed out the obvious—that if she went she would have to find somewhere to live and someone to care for Robin while she worked; that Robin, in her care, would be deprived of his father and, for most of the time, his mother into the bargain. "And I'm not agreeing to him being cooped up in some dreary back room somewhere, and that's all your stage salary would run to," he had reminded her. "I know what it will come down to in the end —one room and some slattern of a landlady keeping an eye on him, if she remembers he's around."

She had threatened to fight for Robin through the courts and he had laughed at her, pointing out she would be the deserting wife and mother and he had given her no cause to leave him.

But she had gone just the same, telling him at the last, "I'll get Robin off you yet, Evan. I'll find a decent home for him and someone decent who'll care for him and I'll find a job and then I'll go to the courts and ask for his custody. You'll hear from me when I've a home for him."

But the only word that had come after that had been on Robin's birthday, when several gaily wrapped packages had come for the little boy. Kiley had engaged a middle-aged woman to act as housekeeper and had tried to settle down in his new role of wifeless father, and now, standing in the deserted house, he wondered in cold rage if tonight was Miriam's doing. It had to be her doing, he told himself. If she could go to the courts and show that Robin had been neglected . . . his mind flicked into mental pictures of the scene in court—of himself admitting that yes, he had had no resident housekeeper at the time—that the latest of several he had taken on had walked out three days previously and the next wasn't due to arrive for a week. And that yes, he had left the boy to the care of a neighbour. That he had done so frequently in fact. That that particular evening he had attended a party where his attendance wasn't strictly necessary. He had gone for the pleasure of company other than that of his son and his neighbour Irene Suttle, and yes, he had stayed out for a long time after the party was over. He could see Miriam's solicitor suggesting that perhaps he had had too much to drink—that he had stopped out so late because he was waiting for the night air to clear his head so he could drive home and appear to Irene Suttle in some condition approaching sobriety.

The worst of it was, he thought in rising panic, that it would be true. He had worried endlessly over Miriam; over how she was faring and how she was living, while refusing absolutely to take the first step towards finding out and seeing her again. There had been the pressure of work into the bargain and the constant anxiety of watching over Robin with only a succession of indifferent middle-aged women to help. He had started drinking soon after Miriam had gone. He had drunk too much by far that night. He had driven slowly, deliberately, towards the vacant stretch of land by the sea and had sat there smoking, waiting till he could go home with some semblance of dignity.

He wondered now how long he had spent there, parked in the middle of the land that had been left him by his father. Kiley's white elephant, Comboroo called it, until a stroke of a government pen on a map and a report had turned it into golden acres.

He had sat up there in the middle of the land that had overnight become worth something like sixty thousand pounds, thinking of plans for Robin and for himself, wondering if the money would bring Miriam back to him, and if it would bring them any happiness if she did come back, while all the time knowing that he still didn't believe his good fortune and that he never would until he held the money in his hands.

He thought now in sudden sickness that if Miriam's solicitors made a good story of his drinking and party-going and possible neglect of Robin, that not even his new wealth might buy him guardianship of his own son.

Now he knew, too, that his stubbornness was repaying him in bitterness. He had deliberately stopped himself from tracing Miriam. Now he hadn't the faintest idea where she was. She could be north or south or west, living in one room or in a country house, and he hadn't a clue to her whereabouts or Robin's, and he wouldn't, until the next day . . . if the voice held to its promise of ringing at midday.

The voice . . . his thoughts caught at the memory and held to it, pulling anxiously at it. It hadn't been Miriam's voice who had said, "We have your son . . ." It had been a man's deep, husky voice, of that he was sure. So who was the man? He felt rage all over again at the thought that Miriam could be shacked up with someone else; that Robin could be in a strange man's arms right then, but the rage went as quickly as it had risen. He told himself not to be a fool. Miriam would never have prejudiced her chances of getting the boy by committing adultery before ever she applied to the courts for custody. She would be living a life of blameless perfection, of that he was sure.

But why had she suddenly risked coming and stealing Robin? And why hadn't she left a note telling him what she'd done? Instead of having someone ring and say, "We have your son . . ."

Abruptly he went back to the bathroom. He bent his head over the basin and ruthlessly turned on the cold water tap, feeling the chill shock of water sliding over his head and neck, dampening his collar and coat and shirt. When he stood upright again, towelling himself as dry as possible, ignoring the discomfort of wet clothes, he knew the last fuddlement of his evening's drinking was gone. He was clear-headed again and thinking rapidly, and the first thing, he told himself aloud, was to make sure there definitely wasn't a note somewhere from either Irene or Miriam. He tried to think of the most obvious place where one would be left—and thought immediately of the nursery.

When he went back into the little cream-painted room the place seemed to strike a chill through his wet clothes. It took some minutes, while he searched through the tumbled cot blankets for a note, to realize he was chilled because the cool storm wind was rushing all through the house from the open windows and doors.

Then he thought of the slate in the kitchen where he chalked up messages for whoever was housekeeping at the moment. Mental pictures jumped vividly to mind again— Irene, with her blonde hair straggling round her face, putting down the phone, running into the kitchen, forgetting whatever it was she had been heating, but lifting the slate pencil and scribbling rapidly, before running out into the night.

The smell of gas was still there, but fainter, when he went back into the kitchen, switching on the light this time, so that the whole room spilt into radiance in front of his eyes, instead of being only dimly visible in the light thrown from the rooms beyond.

So he saw Irene at once. But it took him ten minutes— of untying her from the chair to which she was bound, of stretching her thin body on to the cold orange and grey-flecked linoleum, of talking to her and feeling for a non-existent pulse, before he could admit to himself that she was really dead.

CHAPTER THREE

KILEY said, "I was sure then it wasn't Miriam who had taken Robin. She would never have resorted to violence; would never have dared to tie Irene up like that when it could be later brought out against her in court; when I could stand up and say my deserting wife had violently manhandled the person in charge of Robin and had taken the boy by force.

"Besides, violence, physical violence as distinct from the violence of angry words, simply isn't in Miriam's nature. She wouldn't have assaulted Irene. Of that I was certain.

"And that left ... what?"

.   .   .

He told himself not to be a fool, fighting down the sick gall of panic that was rising in his throat. He told himself over and over again that kidnapping simply didn't happen in this country, while fear was a stabthrust through his heart and mind, reminding him it *had* happened—that only a year previously a child had been taken away and the parents had brought in the police and afterwards ... they hadn't seen their child again. Ever again.

And he was remembering, fear growing deeper, all the publicity about his sudden fortune—publicity that had appeared in his own paper and in the national dailies so that overnight his face and his name had looked out at the world from impressive headlines.

It took him a long time after panic had quietened before he was convinced he couldn't help Irene. Although in life she had never been beautiful, or even particularly pretty, with her olive skin clashing with her fine blonde hair, and her slim body looking at times almost bony, in death she had taken on the garishness of a doll. It was the cherry-red flush of her skin, he realized, that looked as though someone in some childish spite or petulance had spilled a rouge pot over her features.

When he stood up at last he was muttering to himself, telling himself to get a doctor, even while he knew she was beyond any help at all. Her flesh was cold and he found himself debating with a queer, dulled persistency, how long the gas had been flowing out into the closed room and how long she had been dead by the time he returned.

He was sick then, staggering into the bathroom and remaining there till he could shut down on the thought of himself sitting smoking in the middle of the land that had made him wealthy, plotting and planning, while Robin had been taken away and Irene had been dying; till he could cease repeating parrot-fashion, "if I'd come back earlier she'd have been all right. If I'd just come back an hour earlier, say, she'd have been all right and so would Robin."

When he had closed his mind on the unconstructiveness of that he could plan again. He was sure no doctor could help her, so that left the police. He knew the next thing was to phone them and let them swing into the routine that took over when there was violent death.

Then his thoughts blocked on the word police, and refused to go on. In chilling shock he realized that even that help was closed to him. If he rang the police they were going to turn up with flashing lights, in cars proclaiming who they were, in uniforms proclaiming it even louder. They were going to take over the house and himself and Irene's death and Robin's disappearance.

And out in the storm someone had watched the house for the lights to go on and had rung and told him baldly,

"Don't be a fool and go running to the police," and one time before someone had said that to another man who had disobeyed and he had never again set eyes on his child.

The fact that whoever had rung hadn't, surely couldn't have, allowed for Irene's death, wasn't going to help. If the police came it would almost certainly be Robin's death warrant. He tried not to think of Robin—of the boy's plump, rosy cheeks; of the way his hands curled in sleep, and the way he had of laughing through half closed, long-lashed dark eyes. He tried only to think of what he could do for Irene and himself—of some way of handing over responsibility for her, without involving himself and Robin. He rose with feverish haste then, planning desperately as he prowled the room, deciding to take her back to her own cottage, to leave her in the kitchen there, to turn on one of the burners, to let a saucepan of something boil over, to set the stage for an accident, for her to have fallen, say, and knocked herself out so that the saucepan boiled over and the flame went out and she was gassed. In her own house. With no connection between the accident and Robin's disappearance.

He wondered impatiently how long he would have to wait till the gas filled the place, so it would seem feasible she had died there in her own home.

Then his pacing of the room stopped. He knew the plan wasn't going to work. Once he summoned a doctor things would be out of his hands. The doctor would summon the police. The police would come questioning him as a neighbour; as the person who had smelt gas and summoned a doctor to her. And he couldn't afford to have the police anywhere near him. That was the point he had to keep in the forefront of thought.

He lit a cigarette slowly, trying to calm racing thought, knowing that he couldn't simply do nothing. Irene was dead. She was going to be missed, and he didn't know how long it was going to be before Robin came back; before a demand was made for money; before he knew how he was to hand it over and how he was to get the boy back.

He found himself gazing at the phone, willing it to ring, to hear again the man saying, "We have your son," so he could tell him that Irene was dead and that something had to be done about it; that he had to get a doctor and a doctor would get the police. He wanted to assure the other man that even with the police around the house he wouldn't so much as mention Robin's name, when sanity returned.

He wondered what would have happened if the phone had rung as he had willed and he had spluttered it all out. Would the other have destroyed Robin right away? It was only too possible. If he knew that now he might be held for murder if caught, Robin's chances would be slimmer than ever. If the man who had said, "We have your son" thought himself safe he might keep his part of whatever bargain was made and make an effort to return the boy unharmed, with the threat that if even then the police were told, Robin could be hurt in the future.

Memory groped and reflected on rumours he and other newspaper men had heard months ago—that the daughter of a man who had gone from hotel clerk to head of a vast concern in a matter of ten years had disappeared. He had tried himself to probe into the truth of that story. He remembered, with a return of the smarting injustice he had felt at the time, how the door had been slammed in his face and how he had been threatened with a half savage brute of a dog. Remembering, he was suddenly sure the rumour had been true and that the child had been returned, with just such a threat as he had imagined could be applied to Robin's own return.

That way, he reflected, the man could feel smug in a sense of safety and security. But if he knew that no matter if the boy was returned safely the police *had* to be told . . .

What then?

Suddenly he wasn't thinking of Robin, or Irene, or any of the seemingly unsurmountable problems that loomed close ahead for solution. He was trying to work out where a watcher might be.

He didn't believe the man was close to the house. Not in the storm that was raging outside and had been raging all evening. There was no shelter out there and someone in a car on the mountain road wouldn't be able to see far through the driving rain. In any case, if he were close to the house the phone would have rung soon after the grey Holden had stopped by the house, not a good time after, as soon as the lights had gone on and flashed a message out through the night that the owner was home. In any case, he remembered, the nearest call-box was a good distance away.

The Kiley and Suttle homes stood together on Comboroo Mountain. There was another house three hundred yards beyond and still further away a long line of them stretching from the base of the mountain to the sea. The caller might possibly be in one of them, or in the call-box right at the end of the road. Probably there, he reflected. He would be able to see the Kiley house lights spring up and watch the road as well. He wouldn't have been able to be sure, probably, that the grey Holden had been Kiley's when it had shot past. It could have belonged to a visitor to either house, even at that hour. But once he was sure of Evan being home he would watch every car going up and coming down. He would certainly note a police car, or a doctor's.

His thoughts went back to Robin, wondering where he was. Not close by surely. Not somewhere in the district where he might be recognized. So there were two people. One to watch, and one to care for Robin. In any case the man had said "*we* have your son." He refused to admit to himself that the caller might have used the word to mislead and that it would need only one person if Robin was dead.

He went back into the big lounge with its rustling golden curtains and his slow-moving gaze finally fastened on the clock above the huge raw-brick fireplace. Even then, though his mind automatically noted it was now two in the morning, it took time for him to realize his gaze was reminding him that time was flying; that dawn wasn't far off and he had to decide what to do about Irene.

In spite of the sick compassion that urged him to go back to her just once more to make sure she hadn't moved, he couldn't force himself to go back, though he kept reminding himself returning was inevitable as he couldn't leave her there, sprawled in ungainly death. She had to be taken away. And no one must know what had happened until Robin was safely back.

When he tried to think clearly of how he was to manage that, he was appalled. He had lived next door to Irene Suttle for the seven months of her living at Comboroo. She had been a kind of honorary aunt to Robin and another right hand to himself over the past six months, but when he came to think about her he realized she was nothing more than a shadow in his life. She had been about thirty, he thought, a colourless, shy, quiet, introverted woman of faintly slovenly habits. He remembered the way her dresses had seemed sometimes not actually soiled, but faintly grubby and too creased. He remembered the straggling of her thin fair hair and her impatient movements brushing it back. He could remember her speaking of her mother and how the elder woman had died after years of ill health. The house, he could remember that too, had been sold and Irene had drifted to Comboroo because it was close to the sea, and her old home had been far inland. He could remember that, but he couldn't remember the name of the place, or what friends she had had there, if she had ever mentioned them at all. He knew she had taken the empty house next to his on a weekly tenancy and she had made vague plans to sell pottery. She had tried to tell him about that, but he hadn't bothered listening.

Sitting there, trying not to think of her lying so impossibly still, he realized exactly how little he had known about her. She had always seemed competent and willing enough to handle her own affairs—perhaps that had been why, he told himself with sudden relief, he had never tried to penetrate behind the neighbourliness that had appeared to be all she wanted from him.

Then in self accusation he knew the real reason for his lack of knowledge had been simply selfishness and disinterest. He had had his own problems—plenty of them. He hadn't been interested in hers. He knew suddenly that if she had ever really tried to ask his advice or help, he would have cut her short or referred her to someone else.

He walked unsteadily across to the fireplace, peering into the mirror over it. His pale eyes looked back blankly at him. There was an unaccustomed flush on his freckled cheeks, and a lock of hair was lying lankly over his forehead. The lines that Miriam had once dubbed fury lines were deep furrows between his eyes and deeper ones from the corners of his mouth down.

He felt an inane desire to laugh. His son had disappeared and a woman was dead. He was going, in a few short hours, to receive a demand for money. He was entirely on his own, with no one to turn to for help. It was two o'clock in the morning and he had to think of some way of hiding the fact that Irene was dead, for heaven knew what length of time. And all he could do was stare at his reflection and reproach himself that he had never probed into the troubles of someone else who could now never ask for help.

He went to the cabinet against the wall then and deliberately measured out whisky, added soda and drank it. Then he closed and locked the cabinet and put the key into the drawer below, locking that and putting that key behind the books in the shelves beyond the fireplace. It was a trick he had forced himself into in the past weeks in an effort to stop the constant reaching for drinks. By the time he had removed the books, removed the key, unlocked the drawer and removed that key, wisdom had usually triumphed over desire and he was able to measure out the barest minimum of whisky before returning the bottle and locking up again.

He went into the front office then and sat down at the desk, drawing paper and pen in front of him. Deliberately he forced himself to write down Irene's name as the first step in what he thought of as a train of protection for Robin. While half of his mind clutched frantically at the hope that kidnapping was impossible and that it was a trick of some sort, the other half clutched firmly at reason, determinedly plotting how Irene's death could be hidden for hours and days, for as long as was necessary to protect Robin's safety.

In spite of all his efforts, twenty minutes—all he allowed himself for thought—produced very little to help. There was a trail of jottings on the paper and that was all. They read, "Cat. Windows. Spare key. Milk."

He looked at them despairingly. They were all trifles. What about her friends? He didn't even know who they were. Or what she might have planned for the days ahead. He knew as he got up that he would have to move blindly through the future, reaching each possible disaster and turning it aside before it had a chance to trip him.

And the first thing to do was to get her out of his house before dawn.

He was moving towards the bookshelves, his hands

reaching for the drawer key, before he realized it. He almost shouted in rage at himself as he slammed the books back into place. Then he had to waste precious minutes till the rage subsided and he was calm again, calm enough to force himself into the kitchen. He tried not to look at her; tried not to touch her more than was absolutely necessary, as he reached in the pocket of her light cardigan where he knew she carried her front door key. With it in his hand he went back to the office, collected a torch and let himself out of the house, determinedly clutching to himself the belief that whoever had watched him wasn't close to the house and couldn't see his actions. It wasn't till he stood outside that he cursed himself—the house was a beacon of light and situated as it was on the hillside it would be proclaiming to anyone awake that his household was still up. Someone would be sure to see it; to ask tomorrow if something had been wrong in the night, and he couldn't afford questions. He felt his hands shaking again at the realization that someone tonight, seeing the blaze of light, might even have come on up to see if Robin was ill and he needed help. There were plenty of women in Comboroo, masking sheer nosiness under a guise of anxiety for his welfare, who made a practice of prying into his life.

He went running back in, switching off the lights as he went, until one light was left burning alone behind the shaded blinds of the kitchen.

It wasn't till he was walking through the driving rain, with the wind whipping his clothes against his body, that he remembered he wasn't wearing a raincoat and by then it hardly seemed worth worrying about. He didn't dare use the torch for fear the light was noted. He groped his way out of his own front gate and along the fence to the gate and in and up the pathway. He opened the front door and went in, closing it behind him. He didn't switch on any of the lights, but flicked on the torch, holding it low

28

so that light went on the floor and didn't reach the windows. His story, he planned, was going to be that she had been called away to some friend—he didn't know who or where—and she had asked him to care for the huge smoky-grey cat that had once belonged to old Mrs. Cousins who had owned the house and died there. Till the estate was settled the house was rented furnished and Irene had taken over the grey cat along with everything else.

It would fit in with his other story to explain away Robin's absence, he reflected. Everyone knew the latest of his line of housekeepers had decamped. If Irene had been called away, too, it would seem quite sensible that he had given Robin to the care of friends for a while. Because it would be known he had spent the evening till midnight at the party, it might be necessary, he reminded himself, to claim that Irene had taken the boy to friends on her way to her own destination, but he thought that would sound quite feasible too.

He stood, in a minute, against the closed backdoor of her house, startlingly conscious of faint noises. A tap was dripping in the sink against the far wall and curtains rustled, reminding him of his note to shut and bolt all the windows; there were little creaks that made his skin prickle and a faint sound he couldn't put a name to till his torch flickered round the kitchen and he realized it was the purring of the big cat. It was curled up in an ancient wickerwork chair at the far side of the room, its eyes half slits, its feathery tail gently moving. It didn't stir as he opened the back door and went out into the rain again, leaving the door open.

He ran his hand along the paling fence till he felt the hinge that proclaimed the gate. Miriam had made him make it when she had first become so friendly with old Mrs. Cousins. There had been a constant going and coming through it till the old lady had died. Since then he didn't remember that it had been used at all. Irene had moved in a month before Miriam had left, but the gate had remained latched. It hadn't been till Miriam's going that Irene had even entered the Kiley house and then it had been through the front door. The hedge on his own side the palings had been allowed to stretch across it. He had to force his way through, hearing the straying branches crack and break and feeling the wet leaves flutter down round his legs.

Going in through his own back door he left that open as well, then went from the passage into the kitchen. Again he tried avoiding looking at her, but it was impossible and for five frantic, sweating minutes he thought it was going to be out of the question to shift her, or carry on with his plan. For all her thin build she was impossible to lift, to hoist to his shoulder and hold there. Her limbs flopped horribly and when at long last he managed to hoist her so her head hung over his shoulder it was to find her blonde hair straying across his sweating face, sticking to his skin, caressing his mouth, so that he spat and retched in sick disgust, staggering so that he and his burden nearly fell. As he tried to move slowly back to the passage he could feel her thin legs bumping rhythmically in ghostly, playful taps against his own. He hoisted her further forward, so that her head hung down near his waist, and then her long, thin arms flopped forwards and gently tapped his knees. There was nothing he could do to stop it except get the job over before his courage gave out completely.

He went slowly out into the rain-drenched garden again, his burden tapping and bumping with each step, so that each fraction of every second was filled with the monstrous thought of what he was doing. When he reached the hedge he had to take one hand from her to push back the reaching, drenched boughs and her body rolled slightly sideways, the face turning, so that for one moment his eyes, accustomed now to darkness, could see the sheen of her own half open eyes gazing up at him. Hastily he pulled her back, and then her body nestled close against his neck in a dead caress that he tried not to think of as he struggled through the gate and across her dark garden and in through the back door of the house.

With uncertain steps he lugged her into the bedroom. Some remnant of Miriam's complaining voice, "*Must* you always use the bed as a day couch? If you must *can't* you do a little thing like pulling back the spread first?" made him reach for the rose chenille cover and pull it back before he slid her body down.

She fell limply into a position that was strangely like one of sleep, her head half turned against the pillow, one hand outstretched, the other flat against her side, her legs a little bent. He forced himself to straighten her and then to pull up the top blanket at each side and cover her over completely, then fold the rose chenille cover back, so that at last she was only a series of humps beneath the cover. Then he closed the window, bolting it, and closed and turned the key in the door.

The door of her living-room faced him then. He went in and straight to the books that covered one wall and started fumbling at them before he realized what he was doing, and where he was. He began to curse, because the need of a drink was overwhelming and he didn't know where she kept it. He couldn't find anything and went back to the kitchen. There was only cooking sherry and the first taste of it made him sick. He put his head under the sink tap then and towelled himself as dry as possible as he had done in his own house in a time that seemed ages ago now.

He found a piece of card in one of the kitchen drawers and lettered on it in block capitals "No Milk", going on to the front porch to pin-tack it into place, then he groped under the third flowerpot from the front door and removed the spare front door key that Irene had kept taped there. He congratulated himself, as he removed it, that for once her idle chatter had penetrated his consciousness and his memory so that now no one who knew of the spare key could enter the house and find her.

Going back inside he went carefully round the house, testing each window to make certain it was bolted. Finally he went back to the kitchen and hoisted the grey cat into his arms, folding his jacket around it so it wouldn't protest at going through the rain. He felt as reluctant in touching it as he had been in touching its mistress's body—it had become so much a part of Irene in the seven months of her living there that he dreaded taking it into his own house, to have it padding after him through the days ahead, to have it watching him through slitted eyes, to have to touch it and feed it and remember all the time the way Irene's thin hand had stroked at its greyness and how it had weaved and purred round her ankles in the sunshine.

But there was no help for it. Anyone even slightly acquainted with Irene would know that she would never go away without leaving the brute in someone's care.

The last of the reek of gas seemed to be gone when he went in through his own back door. He set the cat down and it went with aloof walk straight into the lounge and stretched out on the blue divan, slitting its green eyes in apparent content, unconcerned with its abrupt change of scene. He left it, forcing himself back to the kitchen, reminding himself he couldn't avoid the place; that at all costs he had to behave normally until Robin was safely back.

Suddenly that was all he could think of. The thought of Irene, of her death, of his own contribution towards it in not coming home sooner, of even the coming days, was swept away in the thought of Robin at that very moment. He was feverishly wondering if the boy was cold, or frightened, or crying; of where he was; of what sort of people had him.

It was a useless exercise in complete demoralization that drove him to the frantic tumbling of books, of unlocking keys and filling a glass with whisky. The drink steadied him slightly. He went back to the office and held his lighter against the page of feeble jottings.

Exhaustion took over then. He went into the bedroom and let himself sink down on the pillows and covers, tearing at his collar and tie till they were loosened, then lying still and quiet. He shut his eyes, trying to will sleep into himself for a long time, till he realized he was listening for the sound of a telephone ringing; that he was willing it to ring so he would have some news, even bad news, of Robin.

CS—C

CHAPTER FOUR

Rain drumming on the roof and gurgling down gutters was a sound gradually seeping into consciousness again when he slowly opened his eyes. The exhaustion still held on to him, but his head moved slowly, his pale eyes focusing eventually on the luminous hands of the bedside clock. It was ten minutes past four and the window showed only darkness outside and the glimmer of water gushing down the closed panes.

He knew he wasn't going to sleep any more—that the little over half an hour that he had had would have to do. He groped for cigarettes, lit up and propped another pillow under his head, then realized his clothes were wet and that he was shivering. Panic touched him again at the thought he might become ill and that when he should be helping Robin he'd be incapable of it. He remembered how the winter before Miriam's going he had had a touch of pleurisy and he tumbled off the bed, dragging his things off to lie in disordered confusion on the fawn carpeting. He padded, naked, still shivering, into the bathroom and stepped under the shower till the heat of the water was sending dagger-jabs of pain through his body, then he rubbed himself dry and went back to the bedroom, pulling on slacks and shirt and pullover, his mind clear again, already planning for the day ahead, striving to see pitfalls, wondering whether the expected phone call would come dead on time or whether the man with the husky voice would use delaying tactics to make the nerve-stretching waiting even more painful; whether he would, when he rang again, give details of how Robin would be returned or whether there would be another delay and another spell of waiting before yet another call, or even a letter came.

He wished suddenly that Robin was older, old enough to speak, so he could talk to him—so he could demand the man bring the boy to the phone, so he could ask Robin himself how he was being treated. Then he was glad the boy was only a baby. As it was Robin was too young to know fear or the terror of sudden uprooting from familiar things. When he came back again he would have no memory to dog him for nightmare days and months in the future.

His thought turned back to the coming phone call; to the possibilities of others; the chance of a letter. And then he thought that Irene must, in the seven months she had lived in Comboroo, have had letters. If she had kept them they might guide him some way. There might be appointments even that she had made for the days ahead.

Almost before he had thought of it, he was throwing a coat round himself and running through the storm to the other house. When he entered the muggy heat of closed-in summer humidity seemed stronger, more oppressive. He went into the living-room and stood there looking about him, walking slowly about, running one finger along the ledge of the bookshelves and seeing streaks of cleanness appear in dust. The room wasn't actually dirty but just, like Irene's clothes had sometimes appeared, a little grubby, as though the very femininity of pride in herself and her surroundings had passed her by.

There was a little desk in one corner of the room. He let the front flap down, expecting a litter of papers, but there were only a few and only two were letters, one a short letter that told him nothing—from someone called Althea. There was neither address nor date on it. It had the vague tone of a letter that didn't expect, or really want, an answer. It was a duty letter, unlike the other. It gave him a cold, dismaying shock when he saw the sprawled signature, "Miriam Stead" at the foot of the blue sheet of notepaper.

Unlike the one from the unknown Althea this had an address—a simple "Kurabana". He found himself totting up distances and realized that Miriam, all unknown to him, had been for some time only about twenty miles away.

The letter was short, but referred to "our last meeting last Wednesday". It thanked the dead woman for some information she had given and reminded her not to forget their appointment with the solicitors the following Tuesday, promising that Irene wouldn't be kept for long. It urged her, too, to ring "if you have anything new" and underneath was scrawled a phone number.

He didn't doubt that the information Miriam had sought and Irene had given had been to do with himself. He felt that he had been stripped naked as he thought of the betrayal that Irene's pose of neighbourliness had hidden all those months.

And Miriam, he thought, had met her several times, according to that mention of "our last meeting". There must have been several meetings before that. A getting-together over teacups in some café probably, he reflected, anger growing. He wondered what stories Irene Suttle had retailed, flicking back her straggling blonde hair with one hand while she toyed with pastries with the other.

Then he realized the date, his gaze on the grey square of window-pane that reminded him it was the dawn of another morning. It was Tuesday right then, he remembered. Sometime in the twelve hours ahead Irene was due at a solicitor's somewhere, to meet Miriam. And what were they going to do when she failed to turn up? Ring and wonder and question why the bell went ringing on and on and was never answered? Come out and hammer on the door, perhaps question the other neighbours, perhaps make trouble?

His hand touched the phone and lifted away, then touched it again and finally dialled. Only when the dialling was finished did he remember the time and realize Miriam mightn't answer. He hoped that she wouldn't, because suddenly he didn't know what he was going to say.

But before he could replace the receiver her voice was in his ear and words gushed out to answer it, "Irene Suttle's dead, Miriam. You've got to come here. There's bad trouble. For Robin, too."

She said uncertainly, "That's Evan . . . isn't it?"

"Yes. You must come," he said and then he put down the phone because he couldn't go on.

In the end, what had happened, he wondered, as he went back to his own house. Had Irene tried to fight whoever had come into the house? He wished that he had looked at her closely so he would have known if she had fought, but he knew he wouldn't be able to make himself go back and find out.

He went back to the kitchen deliberately forcing himself to eat and then with the few dishes washed and dried with a carefulness that a day, a few hours, before, would have made him laugh, there was nothing else to do except look at the phone and expect it to ring, or to stand by the glass wall of the big lounge and watch the dawn come greyly, wetly, to life outside.

At first it was darkness, then the world came slowly into view—the stretch of grey-green grass, of dun-brown earth and two tall palms that was all one could see of the hillside below. One day soon, he had promised himself over and over again, he would have to put up a fence—a tall, strong barrier between the slope of the hillside and the grey curving coast road far beneath it, and an inquisitive toddler. He had planned on chain wire, he remembered, so that the view of sea and sky and passing ships and the white-edged curving coastline to north and south should still be there below the mountain while Robin was safe from danger. Now he wondered if the fence would ever go up; if there'd ever be necessity for it, and he thought suddenly that even if Robin came back he would probably never erect the fence now. He would always remember the sudden sharp awareness of gas and the cold feel of an empty cot and seeing Irene, bound to the overturned chair.

Remembering that, he realized she must have struggled. Probably she had tried to bump the chair towards the gas range so she could somehow jerk the tap down. Only she hadn't made it. The windows had been closed because the tropical downpour had been driving against that side of the house. And the door had been closed too, he remembered. So Irene had been in the dark, with the gas seeping into the closed room and killing her.

He wrenched his concentration back to the world outside, watching the stretch of grass and earth and the two palms come from night-colourless shadow to the greyed paleness of the wet dawn, while the sky edged from dullness to pearl grey. When he turned sideways he could see, out of the corner of the glass wall, Irene's house come slowly to view in the dawn, too. He could see the way the few flowers had been flattened under the solid stream of rain, and how the green paint was fading and flaked on downpipes and guttering. He could see the faint glimmer of dawn light on wet window-panes and with a sudden shiver realized they were the bedroom windows, but he couldn't look away until he heard the sound of a car.

He went out then to the hallway, but he couldn't bring himself to open the door. He was reliving it all, trying to think how Miriam would react, while he waited for the chimes to ring.

The chimes had been Miriam's idea. He had hated them from the first, because their tinkling music seemed at odds with the strength of the brick and stone he had forged into the house, but after her going, he had never bothered to have them replaced.

He wondered what he must look like—if the hours had etched strangeness and wildness into his face—as he opened the door to her because it was as if he had seen a reflection of his own bewilderment and horror in the pale face peering into his.

Miriam spoke as though it were only a moment since they had last talked. "What do you mean, Irene Suttle's dead? What did you do to her?"

It was the last words that shocked him into a spluttering, "What did *I* do to her? Are you off your head?"

"You said she was dead and that there was bad trouble for Robin, too. What did you mean then?"

"Robin's disappeared," he told her baldly and turned away, into the lounge. He didn't look at her as he broke the story to her. When he finished there was only silence and finally he turned to look at her. She was sitting with knees pressed together, her tightly-clasped hands forced down on to them to try and still their trembling, her mouth working. He saw then that she had come in such a hurry that she hadn't bothered to dress properly, or to put on make-up. She looked much younger with her mouth pale and her lashes and brows their natural light brown instead of being darkened. She was wearing a three-quarter brown suede jacket thrown over a black dress and her bare feet were thrust into black sneakers.

He said, "Miriam . . ." quite gently and then suddenly rage against her and Irene's betrayal surged back and he demanded, "Why did you have Irene Suttle spying on me?"

"Because . . ." she began, then stopped.

He demanded impatiently, "What did she tell you?"

She looked up then, her grey eyes considering him critically in a long, steady look. "That you've taken to drinking. That you're half way to being drunk fifty per

39

cent of the time and three-quarters drunk the rest. That's why you can't get a housekeeper to stay in the place. There's always a row about something when you've had a bit too much and then Robin's . . . Robin's all alone again."

Strangely enough he began to laugh. It seemed suddenly absurd—a neurotic grubby little spinster spying and lying her way into Miriam's good graces. For what? For money probably, he thought cynically and wondered idly how much out of her slender resources Miriam had been paying for the information.

He said suddenly, knowing that his laughter had puzzled and shocked and frightened her further, "Forget all that. I found that letter you wrote her . . . no, for god's sake, don't interrupt! I found it and your address and . . . you had a right to know about this. Listen, for a while, at first I thought you'd taken him . . ."

"No! Oh I didn't," she began frantically.

"Don't interrupt," he gave back impatiently. "But when I found her . . . listen Miriam, how much did you know about her? Her friends, the sort of places she might go, the appointments she might have . . ." as she only stared dazedly, he cried, "I've got to cover up her death till Robin's back. Can't you realize that? Listen, don't you see that if whoever has Robin knows he's killed someone he might panic and get rid of Robin?" Then because he was conscious of the brutality in the words he had flung at her, he hurried on, "Listen, Miriam, remember a case over a year ago when a kid went? It was just after there'd been a write-up in the papers about the mother having come into money under some will or other. You *must* remember it!" he stormed at her when she just went on blankly gazing at him. "The parents called the police and the payment they made was never collected and they found the boy later on, dead."

"Of course I remember," she said at last, in a slow, painful voice as though memory was being dragged from her and added to the horror that he had already cast on to her thoughts.

"Afterwards—it was two or three months later I think—though you probably never heard about it, but there was a rumour circling that another child had gone. Right after a write-up in the papers about the father. George Winton, that is. You *must* have read about him." He was storming at her again. "He started off as a hotel clerk and then went into the motel business. There was a heap about him —one paper followed on when the others left off. He's worth plenty. And straight after the write-ups there was this rumour his daughter disappeared. I went out myself and was threatened with a brute of a dog. That's been Winton's answer to all enquiries ever since—a slammed down phone; a slammed door; calling out that brute dog. He got his daughter back, don't you see? That's if she ever went, and she must have, or why doesn't he simply deny the rumours? He paid and stayed silent and that was that. I've got to see Winton. I've got to find out if the girl was all right when she came back. I've got to find out what he learned, if anything, about the people who took her. You're going to come with me, Miriam. You'll have to convince him I'm not only a pressman, but Robin's father, too, and that I'm in the same hell now as he was months ago. It's funny you know," but his voice was mirthless and his face twisted in grief as he went on storming at her, "I've always stood by the press writer's motto that everything justifies a good story and now I'm caught with it. They got hold of the story about my land and the money that's dropped into my lap and they've spread it. And now Robin's gone, and for the first goddamn time in my life I'm realizing what harm a story can do. Go on, Miriam, laugh. Why don't you? It's funny you know. Winton will probably laugh, too."

41

CHAPTER FIVE

GEORGE Winton, looking down at the glowing end of his cigarette, was acutely conscious of the sudden silence from the low, staccato flood of words; was acutely conscious of Annie's blue gaze fixed on him; was more than conscious of the still huddled figure next to Annie, in the armless yellow chair. The girl had a defeated look about her and suddenly he realized her hair wasn't really as dark as he had thought. In the muggy warmth inside the house the disordered tangle was slowly drying to brown. As though conscious that he was looking at her, she slowly raised her gaze, but her grey eyes had a blank look, as though she were coming out of a dream.

He tried to concentrate on her and tried to push aside all the spate of words that had poured over him, because in remembering them, he was immediately drowned in the enormity of the fact that a woman was dead and another child was missing and even if the child were returned the fact would always be there that the woman was dead. He didn't want to consider how far he and Annie were to blame; didn't want to ponder what would have happened if he had spoken out when Victoria had come back to them; didn't want to reflect that perhaps that silence had been a criminal act.

But even while he met the blank grey gaze turned to his, he knew he had to say something and *do* something. He didn't dare look towards Annie as he said at last, "This woman . . . this Irene Sutter . . . Suttle? You're sure she's . . . " and was silent and ashamed of the feebleness of the words.

Evan Kiley said abruptly, "She's dead, right enough. I

tried every way I knew to bring her round. She didn't respond. She was cold anyway. She must have been dead a long time. The cot was cold, too. I left the place at . . . say six o'clock. He could have gone any time after that."

"You said," Winton tried to keep his voice slow and steady, forcing his uneven breath to come slowly and steadily, too, forcing his trembling hands to be quiet, "you wanted to know if Vicky was well when she came back. She was. They didn't even frighten her, so far as we could make out. We had a doctor out straight away and he went over her from head to toe."

He was speaking more to Miriam than to her husband, but she didn't relax and the blank look in her eyes didn't alter.

Then Kiley asked, "How much did you find out about whoever took her?"

"Nothing."

He saw the disappointment and the down-curve of mouth on the other man and said deliberately, "I purposely never tried to find out a thing. Vicky came back. I could afford to lose the money I had to pay out. And . . . we were threatened."

"I thought you must have been. I told you I worked that out, didn't I? Did they threaten to take Vicky again and never let her come back?"

"That, and sending me to hospital a wreck and scarring Annie for life and burning down our home; my motels; everything I had."

"So you didn't do a thing."

Winton's mouth tightened. He sat silent, deliberating over the words, searching in the tone and the words themselves for contempt and bitterness, and then feeling worse because he could find none at all. It would have been easier, he knew, if the contempt and bitterness had been there, so he could feel anger in return and rage at the other man. "What right've you to point scorn at me. I love my wife. Would you want *your* wife returned to you with her face cut to ribbons and her body bruised to pulp? Would you like to come home one evening and find your home burning and maybe your wife and baby trapped inside?"

Annie said abruptly, her voice so low the words were barely audible, "We thought it'd never happen again—that whoever it was'd be satisfied . . ."

"Satisfied?" The word came with a force of a whip cracking over the brown backs of bullocks, and like an animal feeling the goad, Annie flinched and pressed back in her chair as he went on, "Satisfied? When they got away with it so easily once?" Then he shrugged. "To hell with that . . . how was your kid sent back? Did someone drop her off here? Near here? Or did you have to go somewhere and collect her?"

Winton cleared his throat. Looking down at his hands he said rapidly, "We were told to deliver the money and stand by for another phone call. It came some hours after I left the money. They . . . it sounded like a man . . . said Vicky was at Southport. That was a Saturday and there was a surf carnival on there. They told us Vicky was in the lost children's tent. She was. There were quite a few children and only two women in charge. They were too busy to remember who'd brought her in. They'd just accepted the explanation she'd been found wandering on the beach, gave her an ice-cream and a picture book and were sending her description over the loudspeakers at intervals, as with the other children."

After a moment's thought he added, "All the messages we had came by phone. There was nothing written. And the voices . . . I wouldn't know them again. They'd have been disguised anyway, I expect. Wouldn't they?"

"Did you ever go out to see the Griffens—the couple who lost their son and ask them if . . ."

"No," George's tone hardened and he looked steadily, defiantly at the other man. "What was the point? If they'd known about us, they might have put the police on to us. What would *they* have had to lose? They'd want vengeance for their youngster and I wouldn't blame them. They wouldn't bother thinking about Annie getting hurt, or me, or Vicky, or anything else but catching whoever it was killed their boy. No, I didn't go near them." Then, in sudden welling bitterness, he raged futilely into the long, pale-eyed face gazing at him, "and if they had anything to tell, you press people would have printed it long ago. You dredge up everything, don't you, and print it, regardless and . . ."

"That's right. We print it and never think it's telling anyone how much a person's worth, how vulnerable they are and their households are, that they've a kid who could be worth cold cash if taken away . . . listen, how did you pay the money? It was fifteen thousand in the Griffen case I remember. They were to leave it in a twenty-four-hour sixpenny locker on some station, leave the key in the lock and walk away without looking back. Griffen did it, but he'd already told the police by then."

"It was twenty thousand for us. I was to go to Boorool Beach, pay my way into the surf sheds and take a locker; place the money—in a suitcase—inside, leave the key in the lock and walk out. I wasn't to look back, either."

"And you didn't?" There was faint disbelief in the question.

"Would you have? Remembering Antony Griffen? Remembering the way your own baby smiled at you?" He shook his head, slipping off his glasses, swinging them reflectively in his hands, watching the light catch the lenses, seeing tiny pictures in them—of Annie, to one side of him, flame-red hair and simple blue shift dress in miniature; Miriam Kiley, dark and huddled and tinier

45

than ever; Kiley with tiny intent face, winking up at him in glass. "It sounds risky, but it isn't. It would only need two people. One to stand a distance away and watch for anyone lurking around. For the victim to look back. And another to make one quick dash for a key and turn it. And there's another thing, too. I didn't get the message how to deliver the money till it was time to go. I was rung and told to get the money ready and then I'd be contacted again. I had to sit back and sweat. Then they finally rang. Told me to leave right away and go straight to the beach. I wouldn't have had a chance to tell anyone the arrangements even if I'd wanted to and if I'd arranged beforehand to be followed they would have seen me being followed. They planned for everything," he said despairingly. "When I first answered the phone they told me to call to Annie to bring the money to me at the phone; then they told me to call the other women in the house—Vicky's nurse and our housekeeper. I was told to make them run outside—Annie too—and sit in the garden. I was told if they moved or tried signalling to anyone that I might as well have stayed home because . . . Vicky simply wouldn't come home."

"Of course," he added reflectively, "they needn't actually have had a watch on the garden. They'd know the threat would be enough to hold the women."

Kiley reached abruptly towards the green leather cigarette box on the low table beside him, opened it and extracted a cigarette, then made a little gesture of apology towards his host.

"Take one, of course," Winton's voice was suddenly husky as though the long explanation had strained his throat. Then he asked, and knew what the answer would be, "Why did you want to know the arrangements we made?"

"To see if there's some way I could get a line on this

46

mob, without harming Robin. If I could someway be one step ahead of them . . . I thought if I could compare your case and Griffen's, I might see . . ."

"Have you forgotten the way I was threatened. You're sure to be threatened as we were. Are you going to ignore it and go to the police?"

Kiley turned away. He threw over his shoulder, "Have *you* forgotten I have to go to the police—that Irene's dead? Even if that wasn't the case . . ."

"You couldn't sit back, the way I've done?"

He saw embarrassment in the freckled face turned towards him and rage swept over him. Damn him, he thought confusedly, damn him and his embarrassment for what he thinks is my craven-heartedness.

He asked bluntly, "Does that mean you're going to tell the police about Vicky, as well?"

"No. No, you've chosen your road. That I don't agree with it doesn't count. You can talk to the police yourselves or keep quiet. But once Robin's back I'll tell all I can about his going and the more I can tell and the more I can help . . . I thought you might know something to give me a lead because . . ." he rounded on them, his voice raised, a glitter of rage in the pale eyes, "it's not going to happen again. Do you hear? It's not going to happen again. Not ever again!" He took a long breath of smoke, then watched it trickle from between pursed lips before he said in a quieter voice, "How long was it before Vicky came back, George?"

He used the other man's name easily, naturally, and Winton felt a shrinking withdrawal of mind and body. He knew what was the matter, that he didn't want the other man to reach out towards him in friendship and to draw him further into affairs that brought back the long nightmare with renewed force.

When he remained silent Annie leaned forward, big

graceful hands pressed on her knees, her dark blue eyes wide and fixed on Evan Kiley.

"It was a Wednesday when she went. That was always her nanny's day off and I always looked forward to it 'cause it meant getting her on my own. We usually nicked down to the sand with a' picnic lunch and I liked fixing it myself. That morning I settled Vicky out in the garden and went inside again to fix up the lunch before we left. It was the housekeeper's day off too, because of my usually taking her out and George being working and all that.

"I remember I was smiling a bit at her antics when the bell went. I nearly let it slide, but when it went on and on, I went and there was this chap. A Sally he was, rattling a collection box. I said, 'O.K.' and told him to wait just a tick while I got some silver because George'n'me've always given to the Sallies, so I went to rummage for some cash. When I came back, he smiled and said God bless the way they do, and off he went, and I went back to the kitchen and looked out the window. Vicky wasn't anywhere in sight."

Her lips moved soundlessly for a moment. George knew, pain for her a bitter-felt thing in himself, that she was remembering the horror of that morning; then she went on, "I went on out in a real paddy. I was going to warm her backside for her because I'd told her to stay put and she was plenty old enough to understand. And she just wasn't around. Not in the garden, and she couldn't've got round to the road because of the gate George'd put up and it was still latched fast. And she wasn't inside. And she wasn't in the pool. I had to dive in the deep end where the bottom doesn't show, just to be sure. I kept diving and diving and feeling for her and she wasn't there."

Her breath was coming quickly, one hand pressed to her side now, as though she was once more in memory dragging herself exhaustedly from the pool after the last of those dives, her body beaten, her mind working in soaring panic.

She licked at her lips, "I dragged myself in. I was dead beat by then. And the phone was ringing. I didn't even realize I was answering it. I was just wondering where in the name of heaven Vicky'd got to and wondering if I ought to ring the police or George or what, then a voice said, 'Don't go to the police. We've taken your kid away and you'll get her back all right if you play along with us, but if you go to the police . . . that'll be too bad for the kid. Understand?' and that was all, though honestly I don't really remember just what the words were. I rang George and told him and when he came back there was another call, so it looked he'd been followed home, or the house was watched or maybe both, because they wanted to speak to George that time. They told him the price we had to pay. Next time—they never gave us a chance any time to ask questions or even so much as speak—they said how it was to be parcelled up and to leave it ready and we'd hear from them again shortly. Then on the Saturday they told us to leave the money, just as George's said, and a few hours after that the final call came and we had Vicky back again."

Kiley nodded. "This man from the Salvation Army—do you think he was the genuine article?"

"I doubt it," George said and at the question in the other man's eyes, said defiantly, "No, we didn't check to make certain. Annie couldn't even remember what he looked like. He was just a well-known uniform and not a thing more. Annie said he came soon after the women had gone—I expect he'd been checking all our movements for weeks. He'd know the Wednesday routine—the house empty but for Annie, and Victoria out in the garden for about an hour before they went to the beach. They chose their time perfectly."

CS—D

Miriam Kiley spoke in a low, hurried voice, "Then they couldn't have used that way to get Robin, because ... they had to tie Irene up like that and ..."

Kiley spoke without looking at her. "I think they probably kept to the same dodge." He was rubbing one hand over the other, as though his hand was cold, George reflected shrinkingly, as though it still felt the chill of an empty cot, or a dead woman's flesh.

He rasped out, into the muggy air of the room, "What do you mean?"

"I was thinking along these lines ... listen, the house would be closed up wouldn't it, at night? And they wouldn't have been able to get in through a window—I've permanent screens over them. They might have meant to go to the front door and ring. They'd have looked the house over, wouldn't they? Of course they would," he answered himself with a quick nod. "But Irene must have been in the kitchen—they'd see the light there and go to the back door, on to the passage, instead. They'd expect her to go into one of the rooms to get money. When she was gone one of them could have slipped inside and along the passage into the nursery. It would have been easy then to pick up the boy and take him out. There's an outside door to the room—on to a little courtyard affair. It would have bolted of course on the inside, but they'd open it and slip out with him and no one would have been hurt. Only ... " he hesitated and then said wearily, "only Irene was a real Scot."

"A Scot?" George looked at him in bewilderment.

Kiley's pale gaze held impatience. "I mean what people think a Scot is—a tight-wad with cash. Maybe she didn't have much to spend or give away. I never asked. But she never gave to collectors. Especially religious ones. That's one thing I do know about her. She was downright offensive once to a couple of nuns that called. I remember I blew up at her later. She was wild, I could tell, but she didn't let on. She was like that. She bottled everything up. I hardly ever heard her laugh either. She had ... she'd have made her fortune in a poker school with a controlled expression like that ..."

"Oh, that's not true." Miriam had come alive, to lean forward, a bright circle of colour in each pale cheek. "That's not true at all. You should have heard her talk about Robin. She loved him and when she talked about him to me she was ..." her voice trailed off into silence.

In sudden anger Kiley turned on her and demanded, his lips curled back in something that could have been a smile, "How much did you pay her, Miriam? I suppose she played up to you by babbling about what a sweet, dear angelic child your son was. The son you deserted so easily, remember. Didn't she?"

Miriam's voice was a faint thread of sound, "She loved Robin. It wasn't because ... but you won't believe that, and it doesn't matter, does it?"

"No, it doesn't matter," his voice was quite even again. "Now. For the present. But we'll take it up later, Miriam, because I'm going to make it plain to you I'm keeping Robin." Then his face went blank as he finished, "If ever I get him back."

Annie cried out, "You will! We got Vicky back. You remember that. Do you think then that they couldn't get into your house without getting violent and tying up that poor creature?"

"Isn't that what must have happened?" He turned to look fully at her. He went on looking for a long time as though he was really seeing her for the first time; really noting the brilliant flame-red of hair and the wide beautiful shoulders.

George, in spite of himself, felt his temper rising again as the other man went on looking; as Annie returned the look as consideringly as Kiley's own. Then she flushed, looking sharply away, but Kiley kept his intent, considering gaze on her as he said, speaking in a lower voice as though he were talking for her ears only, "Listen, can't you picture it? Irene going to close the door, probably saying something tart in that drab little voice of hers, and the chap putting his foot in the door and whoever was out there in the storm and rain coming to help. Can't you see them shoving Irene back into the kitchen and telling her to sit down and shut up? And then one of them tying her up while the other ran into the nursery and took Robin. They ... you know, before they left they must have told her what they were up to. They'd tell her and warn her about not getting the police, wouldn't they?"

Annie was leaning forward, her face strained, as though she was groping for the pictures he was drawing in the air. After a moment she nodded.

"Yes, I can see it. I guess it happened that way, just like you say. They'd be disguised, wouldn't they? Mind you, a uniform's a good disguise on its own. That's all I can remember. Just the uniform. Silly, isn't it? You'd think I'd be able to put a face on him'n tell you, wouldn't you, but I just can't. Even if I could, I bet the face wouldn't be much like it is now—a bit of sun-tan cream, shaggier eyebrows, a pair of specs . . ." she nodded, "oh yes, I've thought a lot since then; all about how easy it would be to change a fellow's looks."

Winton broke across her voice, asking, "What are you going to do?"

Evan Kiley didn't answer straight away. He still looked at Annie as he desperately at last replied, "What else can I do but go home and sit by the phone and wait for that next call?" He rounded suddenly on the other man. "That's all there is to do, isn't it, George? It's what you had to do, too. Sit down, as you put it, and sweat. And

God, how you sweat! Don't you?" He shook his head. "I shouldn't have come here, stirring it all up again for you, involving you like this, but I thought . . . I hoped there was some way I'd get a line . . ."

"If I could help you, I would," Winton broke in and his voice, he knew, mirrored the agony in his mind as he remembered all over again that this man's sweating and the woman's pain; a child's disappearance and a woman's death, could possibly be laid at the door of his own conscience. If he had spoken out long ago the people might not have been caught, in spite of all the police could have done, but they wouldn't have dared try again for a long time, if ever. They wouldn't have read in a newspaper about a man who had become well-off overnight and, because they had had easy pickings before, decided to strike again. He asked, "Do you think this Irene Suttle will be missed? What are you going to do about her?"

"What can I do there, too, except sit tight and sweat it out and deal with everything that crops up as it comes?" Kiley thrust out his hands despairingly, then gazed blankly down at the upturned palms. "It makes me sick to my guts to leave her there, but what else . . . I've got to keep the police clear of the mountain and myself."

"If I could help . . ." Winton began and realized the futility of the words.

"You can't help there at all, but . . . it would help to have someone to talk to—someone who's been through it all—to tell about each call, to . . ."

"I know. I know just what you mean," George agreed eagerly. "Call me. Any time. If you want me, too, I can come on out."

Kiley nodded. He didn't speak again, only crushed out the tiny stub of cigarette that was left in his fingers and walked towards the door. After a moment Miriam rose and followed him out. Her shoulders, under the brown suede jacket, were slumped. Her feet, in the shabby sneakers, dragged. She didn't speak either. At the front door Kiley turned. He looked full at Annie again. He didn't say anything but Annie flushed again, looking away. Then Kiley moved on out and the girl moved to follow, but as Kiley had done, she paused for an instant. Her gaze flicked back. Not at Annie. At himself. Her eyes were wide and darker than before and frightened and lost. Instinctively he put out a hand to her. She didn't touch it, but a little smile touched her pale mouth for a moment before she turned and ran lightly out to join her husband in the grey Holden.

CHAPTER SIX

ANNIE was out in the play-room, reading to Victoria, when the phone call finally came. She had wanted him to ring Kiley as the minutes had dragged by, but he had reminded her that whoever was phoning Kiley might be deliberately stretching the man's nerves further by delaying the call. She had given in at last, going in to Victoria and he didn't call her when the phone finally went and he heard Kiley's voice again. He only asked eagerly, "Have you heard?"

"Yes, George."

As before he felt the faint sense of withdrawal at the use of his christian name; at the quick reaching out to draw his friendship close to Kiley's concerns. Deliberately, fighting against the withdrawal, he forced himself to say, "Evan, we were worried. They let you sweat it out for longer than you counted on, didn't they?"

"No. No, the call came dead on midday just as they promised, but ... I'll explain in a minute. First though, the call itself."

"Yes?"

"It's twenty thousand."

"In single bills? It will take a bit of doing, you know, to get hold of them without having the bank making polite enquiries as to what you're up to. Annie and I've always thought since that it was me having to ask for singles that started the rumours. Some youthful teller talked a bit, we consider. Probably thought I was on to some big deal with the other chap trying to dodge tax. Not that it matters of course. Sorry I keep babbling ... Evan."

"It doesn't matter. I haven't had any instructions yet. Just the price."

"And the boy?"

"O.K. They say."

There was silence for a moment. Winton knew that Kiley was thinking, as he was himself, that the word of a kidnapper wasn't much to hold on to. But it had to be held on to, or Kiley would go crazy in the hours ahead.

He said rapidly, "Remember that Vicky came back to us in good shape. Hold on to that. And it will help a bit now you've something to do—getting the money together I mean. You'd better ask for single bills right off. That will help save time. If you get big notes you're almost certain to find they want singles. I shouldn't think they'd dare take anything bigger."

"No, no I guess not. George, do you like cream cake?" There was a faint sound over the line that could have been a snicker of hysterical mirth.

George heard it, blinking his surprise at the wall in front of him. He said, "Cream cake?" on a note of wonder.

"Yes, cream cake, George. The bakery van came a while ago. I'd forgotten about that. I don't even know what she took. Irene, I mean. But I saw the man go up and knock. Later on he came here. And George . . . I just wasn't game to open the door. I thought, what if they think I'm passing on a message to him to get the police? So I stayed quiet. Listen, George, it got me thinking—I could have put a note in one of my empty milk bottles last night, couldn't I? Telling the police to ring me because they couldn't have my phone tapped surely to god, now could they? I thought there were so many ways of getting a message over it seemed they were running incredible risks and then . . . they're not, you know. Put out a note and I couldn't count on someone not talking, whispering. Could I? I've thought up a dozen ways I could get messages sent and receive them, too and then it all boils down to the fact someone else would be involved, someone

56

else would know and they might whisper—because Robin isn't theirs and it'd make such a story . . ."

"I know," George broke in eagerly. For once he and the younger man were linked in complete understanding. "When Vicky went it was the same with us. We thought of sending a message through one of the tradesmen or through a casual caller and then . . . we couldn't risk it. People would swear themselves blue in the face they wouldn't let out a whisper and then . . . it would be just one unguarded moment with a person *they* thought was safe and then the whisper would spread and grow and not anyone who passed it on would mean to harm Vicky but they would, just the same. Even with the police—there'd have to be a lot of them knowing . . ."

"No, while Vicky was gone you couldn't go to the police," Kiley said evenly. "I see *that*."

The little stress on the last word was like a blow in the face, reminding that Kiley couldn't see or understand the rest, the continuing silence when Vicky had come back.

Then Kiley said abruptly, "Where was I, anyway? Oh, the cake. Do you think she's expecting visitors, George? When the bakery van went, I went out for a look-see. He'd left my usual loaf and for Irene he'd left a half and a box. I opened it. It's a cream cake. That must mean there are visitors coming, mustn't it?"

"It might just mean she liked cream cake," Winton said heavily. He felt his stomach churning at the idea of the woman selecting and ordering a cake, with death hovering over her shoulder.

"Well you might be right at that, George." Kiley's voice was lighter. "Not that I'd know. To me she was a silly, rather grubby, down-at-heel, nosey spinster. And," his tone was suddenly angrily mocking, "you think I'm a bastard to say so, don't you? But just remember she spied

57

on me and that makes her worse to me than any tart off the streets. Get it?"

George didn't comment. He only asked, "Is your wife with you? How's she standing up to . . ."

"She's gone home. To rehearsal. Didn't you know, George, that the show must go on; that good troupers don't cry and a whole heap more of traditional crap? No," he amended sharply, "that's not fair. I told her to get out. I told her to go. And you think again I'm a double-dyed bastard, don't you, for doing it? But I had my reasons, George. What's the use of her sitting here and waiting? There's nothing for her to do except fight with me and I'm in the mood to fight, I can tell you. She's better off sinking herself into her work. What I'm wondering is what she'll do when Robin's back. Is she going to fight me for custody? Does a dead woman's word count in court, George, do you know? Does her word about me being a drunkard and a neglectful father count, George? That's what dear Irene was going to put her name to, George— that I'm a drunkard and neglect my baby son."

"Shut up," George said quietly over the spate of words.

The funny little snicker sounded again and George felt his flesh prickling in acute distaste. Had the other been at the bottle, he wondered, before revulsion against his disgust reminded him he had no right to blame Kiley for seeking what solace he could. He had nothing else to turn to. It had been bad enough when Vicky had gone, but Annie had been there, Annie with her fierce, "She'll come back, love. Oh, George love, she'll come back. Hold me tight, George love, and don't you worry. She'll come back."

Kiley said abruptly, "Thanks, George. If I start off in that tack again just say that again, will you? Just tell me to shut up." Then he added quickly, "Listen, George, I want to see you. I've got to ask your help . . ."

The elder man felt a curious lightening of spirit, as though the help he would give would be some measure of atonement. He heard his own voice babbling eagerly across Kiley's, "Of course, of course, you know I'll help. Anything at all I can do . . ."

"You mightn't be so eager, when you hear. Could you come on out anyway and listen to me?"

.   .   .

George drove slowly through the town of Comboroo, noting the huddle of old weatherboard and decaying brick at the far end of the town and the smarter modernity of the few shops nearer towards the mountain and the sea. The place had an air of slumber, from the thin ribbed dogs dozing in the now bright sunshine, to the shopkeepers leaning against awning uprights and chatting while waiting for something to happen. He had seen the thin-arched stretch of silver-pale sand further out with the bright blue of sea, still churned to high waves from the recent storm, rolling in in white capped breakers, but he could see also why the town had never become any bigger. The deep cove that cut in in the south and circled round behind the town almost cut it off into an island and there was only a single-track bridge going across it. He could see how the rumoured government plan of a new highway and a four lane bridge would sweep traffic off the main highway further inland and bring prosperity and new life to the whole place. He wondered as he drove slowly past a small building with a large, brightly painted sign *Comboroo Times*, where the land was that had turned Kiley overnight to front page news. Then he saw the turn for the mountain road and found himself almost envying Kiley in his solitude and his view and in the long, low house that perched there beyond a white picket fence. Then, as he stopped the car, his gaze slid sideways and he could see the flaked paint

59

on guttering and downpipes that Kiley had mentioned. The house there was of weatherboards and much older than Kiley's. It was set further back from the roadway, too, and the garden was neglected.

He shivered slightly as he looked at the closed, curtained windows, then he turned his back on it. He went up the path to the newer house and the door opened to frame Kiley, with behind him a grey cat weaving sinuously towards his legs. As the animal touched him, Kiley flinched away, looking down.

He said wearily, "The brute's hers," and bent to grab at it. "I don't want it getting out again." He led the way inside, tossing the cat on to the chair by the fireplace before turning to his visitor to say curtly, "That's one thing I want to ask of you. Will you take the brute away with you? I don't mean," he added impatiently, "destroy it. It hasn't done any harm, god knows, but it keeps getting out and going over there and scratching at the door . . ." the tip of his tongue licked at his lips, "as though the brute knows. I have to go fetching it back and . . . well I can't stand it, that's all. If anyone asks where it is I'll say she took it with her, that's all. You don't have to keep it round your place you know—you could find a home for it somewhere."

George looked out through the glass wall at the almost incredible view of mountainside and sea and silver-pale stretch of sand. He knew suddenly, with a feeling akin to complete despair, that he disliked Kiley. Came close to hating him, in fact. Yet he knew that if they had met in the normal course of events they would probably have struck up a casual, easy friendship of sorts.

He knew that the dislike had its roots in the fact that Kiley had drawn him back into a nightmare he had long thought over for good; for drawing him further and further into the heart of darkness and despair. He didn't want to ke the cat, or even to touch it, and when he turned round he knew from the look in the pale eyes turned to him that Kiley knew it too.

The younger man said shortly, "Here," and thrust a glass into his visitor's hand, then said, holding his own glass up to the light, "Whisky for you, ginger ale for me. I *can* keep it sensible, you see."

"I'll take the cat of course," George said abruptly. "Do you own the *Times*? I passed the building driving up."

"No. A bloke called Crest does. He's in the late seventies. I intended to buy it whenever it came on the market. I've been editor for some years."

"I shouldn't have thought a town this size would run to a paper of its own," Winton said idly.

"It wouldn't if there was another local paper in the area. Crest started it as the *Times* in Panuni, further inland. Then he was told to get to the sea for his health and moved lock, stock and barrel out here, switched the name and kept on building up the circulation. It's not a bad rag you know," his tone was a little too casual, as though he was fighting down a tendency to boast. "We do the usual society jottings for the women; but we concentrate on international affairs and fiction and on the bigger stories— we've had plenty of scoops that the big city dailies have been glad to take up second-hand."

"Stories like Vicky's going?"

"Yes. I tried getting that. I would have tried again later on when your guard was starting to relax a bit. I'm being honest, you see. But listen," he downed the last of his drink and pushed the empty glass aside, "I need your help."

"I told you . . ."

"That's what I'm counting on. Listen George, they've asked me for twenty thousand and I'd pay double that for Robin's safety . . . if I had it. But I haven't. I haven't twenty thousand either. Or ten thousand. Or five thousand. I doubt if I can raise one thousand in a hurry."

"But I thought . . ."

"Yes, that spread made it seem everything was settled, didn't it? That I had sixty thousand in my fingers right now. But I haven't, George. Oh, I think it's square enough the government is going to build a highway and four lane bridge to take the main stream of traffic off the highway, but . . . after the rumour first hit and the press spread it and pointed out Comboroo was all set for a building boom as a tourist resort and that I, owning all that land . . . come over here and I'll show it you . . . look down there, all that stretch near the sea—you can just see it from here . . . that's all mine . . . I'd be able to sell it for just about any price I named—after that the government denied the plans, just as they've done in other cases like this. I suppose it stops speculators moving in and buying up everything cheaply and making a killing later on in which the original owners don't share.

"But I can't go hawking my land now. In any case it would take time to sell it all. One of the articles said I'd been offered sixty thousand and that's true enough. I've been on to the people who offered it. You can check on them, Triangle Investments, but I couldn't tell them why I had to have the money now and they won't play till the day the contract for the bridge and the highway is signed.

"So you see how it is. I haven't got twenty thousand yet. Just that land, and I'm damned sure these swine, whoever they are, aren't going to listen and give Robin back to me for nothing." He saw the elder man's gaze move slowly round the room and said shortly, "The house is mortgaged to the hilt. I was a bloody idiot to build it. Miriam wanted it. A dream home she called it, and I wanted to satisfy her, but even a dream home wasn't good enough to keep her here. Yet you know what, George?" his pale eyes had a blank, unseeing look, "I still love her. I've tried hating her, and it hasn't worked, and I keep wondering if *I* was the wrong one after all, or what? Oh what the hell!" he shrugged the words aside, "life's crazy, anyway, isn't it? Anyway I raised a mortgage on this place that'll take me a lifetime to pay off. Even the furniture . . ." he snickered again on the note Winton had heard before, over the phone, "even that's on the never-never. I don't know how much of it I own — perhaps a leg of that chair near you and maybe the top of that table over there, but lord knows. I do own the car. That can go. I might get seven hundred for that. And there's a few shares — I anticipate two hundred, maybe a bit more, on them, providing the market's good right now.

"But the bank will have to give me the rest. The land sounds good security, but I'm wondering if they'll think so. Remember the government's denied the plans for the moment and I can't expect a retraction to please me, can I? I remember all the trouble I had raising finance for the house — I felt I'd been put through the wringer by the time I was finished and . . . it took time. Time, George," he turned desperately to the other man, "I haven't got it. I can't let Robin stay in their hands all the time I'm praying and pleading and begging for money. And I doubt if they'd wait long, anyway." His face was grey when he asked bluntly, "Will you stand guarantee for me? With the bank? I know it's asking a lot, but the land's there and it's all mine. I can't believe the plans won't go through, but banks don't work on rumours, George. They deal in facts. So my only hope is you'll stand guarantee. It's a risk for you, of course. If it doesn't pan out, you'll have to re-pay the bank and all you'll get in return is a strip of land that *might* come good some day if the government change their minds yet again."

When Winton remained silent he said incredulously, "My god, you're not going to do it. Are you? You won't risk it. You . . ."

"Don't be a fool." George's face was white with anger. "You know I'll do it because you know I'm hating myself, that I'll have to live all my life out knowing that woman is dead and your son was taken because . . ." he stopped, turning away again to look out through the glass wall. Then he said evenly, "If you go to the bank I doubt if you'll get it without a fair delay. They'll want to check on me thoroughly. No, the simplest and best way is for me to give you the cash on the security of the land—for me to play banker."

He suddenly smiled. He felt relief, sweet, comforting relief as he stood there. It was as though, because he could do this, he was making some retribution for what had happened. He wondered if Kiley understood, as the man remained still, gazing at him intently.

When Kiley didn't speak, Winton said urgently, "it's no more risky. Either way I might lose my money, but . . . it doesn't matter. You understand, don't you?" he was suddenly pleading. He didn't want to have to put how he felt into words, to make the abjectness of confession at his hatred of himself and how the offer of money would help him as much as it would help Kiley to accept it.

Then abruptly the younger man nodded. His lashes lowered over the pale eyes as he said, "I understand."

Winton's shoulders straightened. He felt somehow immeasurably taller. Taking off his glasses he began polishing them painstakingly on a handkerchief that he noticed with faint surprise was amazingly dirty. He found himself speculating how it had ever got into such a condition, then remembered these grey slacks were the ones he had worn the previous day when he had been playing with Vicky and she had been dabbling in paint. He had wiped her small starfish hands on his handkerchief.

Vicky, he thought, and a knife of pain twisted in his heart. He said swiftly, "That's settled then . . . Evan. The cash is yours as soon as I get hold of it. I don't anticipate any trouble. My bank account's healthy and though most of my cash is tied up my bank won't quibble about an overdraft. They know me."

"Then I'll see a solicitor. Have the land made over to you."

"There's no need for that, there's . . ."

"Yes there is," Kiley said tightly and swiftly. "You're to have the land. For twenty thousand. No, say nineteen thousand, a few hundred more maybe. Whatever is left after I've disposed of the car and my shares. I'll sell you the land for that and then the risk is all yours."

"That's crazy," Winton protested. "The land is worth much more if the highway goes through and in any case . . ."

"I don't want more from you than that. And I want it legal."

For a moment the two of them stared at one another in silence, then slowly the dark red of anger flooded up into Winton's cheeks. He wanted to lash out at the other man; wanted to rail at him and strike at him.

Instead he said quite evenly, "So now we understand one another. In spite of your talk you hate my guts, don't you, Kiley? You'd like to smash my face in. You think I'm a coward, don't you?"

Kiley said tightly, "Yes. A stinking coward. It's no use bucking it, is it?"

"No, but . . ." in spite of himself there was faint pleading in his voice, "put yourself in my place. If your wife had been threatened . . ."

"I'd feel I was man enough to look after her. Being prepared for something—knowing there's danger ahead . . . it's different from this sneaking business of stealing a kid. Oh to hell with it!" In sudden violence the younger man blundered away towards the cabinet, reaching for the

CS—E

whisky bottle and a glass, splashing the liquid into it. He said thickly after a moment, "I never meant you to know how I felt. I've tried my damnedest to see your point of view, but . . . I don't. But I need your help. Are you going to give it, now I've told you what I think?"

"Yes. You're entitled to think what you like."

"And entitled to name my price and have everything legal?"

Winton turned away from the window. He felt quite calm again. In fact he knew it was a relief that Kiley no longer pretended to friendship. "I'll get in touch with my bank and lawyers if you'll see yours. Have you a basket for the cat? If I put it in the car it'll almost certainly jump out again."

"I'll fix it."

When Kiley came back he was sucking at a long scratch on the back of his hand and carrying a wicker lunch basket. He said shortly, "The brute took a swipe at me. Watch your face when you open the basket. And look—take the cake with you, will you? It's sitting there, leering at me."

Winton said abruptly, "I shouldn't have come here. I was just thinking what you said about passing on messages. They . . . if they're watching they'll have seen me arrive. What if they think I'm something to do with the police, or that I'm taking a message?"

"Not if it's the same crowd who took Victoria they won't. I feel safer having had you here. Forgotten they know you, George?" The voice was faintly mocking. "You didn't call the police. Then. Or after. You were a good little boy. They'll feel sure you'll urge me to play along, as you did. They got off scot free then, didn't they?" The mockery was lost in sudden anger, "And they're still free. Aren't they, George?"

CHAPTER SEVEN

WINTON had a feeling of flatness, of unreality, as though the hard bright sunshine was a stage set and he was a ham actor forgetting his lines. He had stopped the car on the sea road above a stretch of brown rock whose pitted surface was filled with salt sea puddles from the last high tide. The grey cat had been restive for some time before that, calling and crying and scratching at the basket till it had frayed at his nerves. He spoke to it, with the car halted, while he lit a cigarette and wondered what to do with the animal. Taut-stretched nerves urged him to undo the clasp of the basket and let it free, deserting it, but revulsion against the idea, the fear that it might die a lingering death, and that he would be guilty of an act of complete cruelty stopped him, but he knew that its presence in the house would be a constant goad to both himself and to Annie, reminding him with every soft pawing at them and glance from green eyes, of Irene Suttle. Unreality stole over him again as he thought how the unknown woman had become so deeply entrenched in his life. He had never met her, never touched her hand or looked into her eyes, but he knew that for the rest of his days she would always be there in thought.

He spoke again to the cat and it answered with a faint growling call and was still again. His gaze fell on the box then. He could see a little spot of grease against the side of it. He thought in relief that that at least was one thing he could desert without worry and a few minutes later he watched the cardboard box sink slowly into the sea.

·　　·　　·

67

He stood for a moment blinking in the late afternoon sunshine. He could see Vicky, in an absurd minute polka-dot blue bikini splashing energetically in the pool with her water-churning version of the dog paddle, while four-year-old tow-headed Timothy Parks from along the road watched her with an expression compounded of envy, admiration and sheer green-eyed jealousy. He felt an uplifting of heart, a desire to chuckle, to run down to the pool himself and take Timothy under his wing, teaching him to outshine Vicky just to take her down a peg or two.

Instead he walked to where Annie was stretched out on the white cushioned cane lounge, watchful gaze behind dark glasses fixed on the two children. She was wearing jewel-bright tight green slacks and wild-yellow blouse that was looped and tied in front, leaving her waist bare. Her feet were bare, too and her flame-red hair was half covered with a huge-brimmed straw hat of whirls of bright green and yellow and orange. She should have looked impossible—instead she looked beautiful—completely at one with the hard sunshine and the bright world of the coast, like the many-hued parakeets that rested among the scarlet poinsettia trees.

She said, seeing him, "George," and made his name sound a caress and a welcome together. Her bare white arms went round him for a brief moment, then she asked, "What happened?"

He told her, sitting on the cane lounge beside her, arching one arm over her while he talked. She didn't interrupt, fixing her gaze on the children again. Then she said, "It helped, you being able to get him the cash, I mean. Didn't it? To make you feel better?"

"Yes."

She nodded, turning to face him again. Her hands went up either side of his cheeks, pressing there as she asked, "George, what if he brings us into it? Spills all he knows

68

about Vicky going, as well as about his little kid? I know he promises to keep quiet, but promises're easy to make, easy to break, aren't they, love? And I know enough of men to know he's the type'd go all out for getting even, if he's hurt. He'd just set his heart on putting things square and let heaven look after anyone who got in his way innocent-like."

He put his own hands over hers, to draw them down in a tight clasp against his body. He said slowly, "I'll tell in any case, Annie. I couldn't stay silent. Not after this, and maybe have it all happen again to someone else. Not that we can tell much, but they . . . the police . . . they'll want to compare our case with Griffen's and with Kiley's . . ."

She nodded. "I thought you'd say that. Oh you needn't worry, love. I couldn't keep my mouth shut either. To live through this all over again . . . you know, it all makes it worse that I'm really thinking about you and me all the time and not the Kiley pair or that poor kid or . . . or that woman. I keep saying to myself, I'd never live through it happening again, and it's me I'm thinking of, not someone else suffering . . . you understand what I'm getting at and trying to say?"

He nodded.

She asked abruptly, "Where's the cat?" not looking at him, so that he knew she was afraid he had it somewhere close; that soon she would have to listen to its voice, counter the watchful gaze of its green eyes and have it padding at her heels.

He told her, "I left it at a little tea-room. It was a clean little place, and the woman looked kind and there was an older woman . . . probably the younger one's mother . . . sitting out in the sun in a little garden at the side. The place was attached to a filling station. I expect," he didn't know why he was going into so many details, but he couldn't stop the eager flow of explanation, "I expect the younger woman's husband runs the garage part and she runs the café and the mother just nods in the sun and helps perhaps with a little washing-up. There didn't seem to be a cat about, or a dog either. Or even a bird that might mean they wouldn't want a cat around the place. I let him out of the hamper and put him just inside the fence round the garden. No one saw me . . ."

He spoke in self-congratulation, believing the statement to be true.

. . .

At five thirty the phone went again. This time Kiley's voice seemed rasping, as though his throat was tired; as though he had been speaking and arguing with someone for a long time before he had rung.

He said without preamble, as soon as he heard Winton's answering voice, "I've sold the car. I'll need it almost certainly for delivering the payment won't I? So I made an agreement I keep it for one week, but get the cash for it now."

"You could always have borrowed mine, or our station waggon."

"Thanks, but no."

Winton felt again the blaze of anger and resentment at the other man's attitude. He crushed it down to say quite evenly, "Is there anything else I can do?"

"Let's drop that for the moment. I'll need nineteen thousand one-fifty. How does that strike you?"

"Crazy. The land's worth much more."

"Let's not argue the point." Kiley's voice was tired now. "Nineteen thousand one-fifty's my price for it. I'm going to lose on the shares — they've dropped, but it can't be helped."

Winton began, "but there's . . ." then stopped, because he knew his protest would do no good; would only bring the tightness and hardness back into the other man's voice again. He said, "Nineteen thousand one-fifty, then," then felt a smooth strong hand over his own. Annie's voice said in his ear, "Let me," and when he released the receiver to her she asked urgently, "Is there any news of Robin?"

"Hello, Annie . . ." George, his ears pressed close to Annie's, felt anger again at the sudden warmth in the voice, that told the other man had no contempt for Annie; indeed liked her very much. "I had a brief message. The swine didn't even give me time to ask about Robin this time. He just said, 'It's to be single bills. You'll be told later on where to send it,' and put down the phone his end and left me to sweat. Was it that way with you?"

"Yes." George felt a shiver run through the big beautiful body beside him. "Just that way."

"I wanted to listen closely to the voice, but it seems different each time. The first time it was deep and husky — I doubt if it could've been faked by a woman. Next time it wasn't so deep. This time — I don't know. It could have been either sex."

"It sounded like a man right along, with us."

"Annie," his voice was urgent, "Couldn't Vicky tell you anything at all when you got her back? She must have been old enough to chatter a bit."

"A bit?" Annie suddenly chuckled, "Bless you, a television commercial isn't in it with her for cramming a hundred words into one minute, but all she could talk about was the big cake they gave her — trust her to think of her stomach — and then she went to sleep. They doped her, you see and . . ."

"Doped!" Kiley's voice was almost a yell. "You didn't tell me that. You said she was all right."

"She was!" Annie cried over his voice. "She was! The doctor said she wasn't hurt at all, but she'd had some dope put into her by the look of her and the sound of what she said."

George abruptly took the receiver back. He said curtly, "Kiley, remember that Robin's only fifteen months old. He can't talk, so it wouldn't matter what he saw or heard. So there'd be no reason for doping him."

"A baby can howl blue murder. Robin has lungs like a foghorn," Kiley said tightly. "And he's fifteen months, just as you say. A baby still. Dope might . . . kill him."

"You're just torturing yourself. You'll crack if you keep that sort of thing up." George was suddenly seeing the cabinet in the big glass-walled room, and Kiley alone in the silent house with nothing to do but pace up and down and look out through the glass wall at the house beside him. He asked sharply, "Kiley, what about your job?"

"What about it? Oh, I see . . . I've plenty of time owing me and I want to keep out of town. Remember us talking about passing on messages? I don't want *them* to get any idea I'm playing ducks and drakes with Robin's safety and I know too many people who'd wonder what I was up to if I passed them without a word. And that goes for our local copper, too."

"So you're alone in the house? Well I'm coming over. I'll throw a few things into a bag and I'm staying over with you till Robin comes back."

There was silence, then Kiley said, "I'm supposed to be grateful, aren't I? And I know why you're offering, but . . . let's be frank. I don't want you under my feet. That's all there is to it. Besides . . . I'm going to ask your help in another direction. You *did* offer any help . . ."

"Well?"

"Perhaps you'd best come here and I'll explain in person. I don't want to leave here now. Two reasons, the first being another message might come. I don't want to delay getting it. Second reason—next door."

"Both valid," George said as curtly. "Shall I come now?"

"What suits you suits me. I've nothing to do but sit and wait."

.   .   .

Annie got out of the car first. She was still wearing the bright green slacks and had added high-wedged yellow scuffs to the outfit, but her flame-red hair was bare. It shone even through the dusk of a storm-clouded night. There were no stars, only the promise, in deep rumblings away out over the sea, of a storm to come, and the muggy heat was worse than ever. She slapped angrily at her bare arms as she stood peering towards the lighted Kiley house.

She said absently, "The devil must have sat on a hot coal the day he invented mosquitoes."

Winton didn't smile. He said heavily, "We're here," and stepped out to stand at her side, whistling the big dog to heel. Margold had jumped into the car as they were leaving the house and Winton was glad now. It gave him a feeling of safety against watchers in the night on the mountainside to have the big Alsatian there at his side.

"Yes, we're here." Annie swung round on him, clutching at his arm with one hand, her fingers digging in hard to his flesh. "George," her tone was one he had rarely before heard her use, "I'm frightened," she told him simply.

He tried to see her features through the dusk, but couldn't. There was only the flame-red of her hair, slightly dulled by the shadows, and the pale oval of face and that was all. "I'm frightened," she repeated.

"Of Kiley?" he asked in bewilderment.

"Don't be a nut!" She gave him a shaky laugh, then said slowly, "but maybe you're right at that. I guess I'm frightened of what he'll do. I'm scared of what he's going to talk you into."

"He can't make me do anything I don't agree with."

"Yes, he could," she said flatly. "In your present mood

73

he could talk you into flying to the moon and you'd do it because you're sodden with guilt. Aren't you? You keep needling yourself it's all your fault and you want to do everything he says, to try and make up. George, don't be a fool, love. Please. Don't say yes, and go blindly ahead. Because it mightn't be the right thing to do. It might cause trouble and ... if things go wrong ... you'll go mad with blaming yourself after. Won't you?"

He knew she was right—that he'd come with the idea of falling in with Kiley's plans, however fantastic they might turn out to be. He hadn't looked for the trap that lay in wait for him if the plans were foolhardy and went wrong.

He said, and suddenly felt a shiver of fright go through his body, "I'll watch it, Annie."

He went up the path and rang the bell. The chimes sounded sweetly through the night, but they weren't answered. He let them sound again. And once more, before sheer panic took over. He said, "There's something wrong. He wasn't going out. He was afraid another message would come. Annie ..."

"Hush, then ..." she might have been speaking to Victoria, but he was in too much of a panic to resent it. She said, "Go round to the back."

He didn't want to, and the very pitifulness of his reason was another goad to his mind, because he knew he didn't want to go to the back door through which Irene Suttle's body had been carried by Kiley. He didn't want to touch it, or see the kitchen where she had died.

He knew he would only achieve some sort of self-respect if he went. He said, and his voice croaked so that she turned to peer at him, "Yes, I'll go. You stay here in case he comes."

He found a concrete path leading round the side of the house. He went quickly, the big dog padding silently at his side, and as he rounded the house and faced the back

74

of it, he could see the door was open and light was spilling out over a small concrete terrace. He stopped and whispered, "Kiley . . ." though he knew his voice couldn't have carried more than a few yards; and certainly not through the open doorway.

Then he saw the flickering light that showed for one instant behind the shuttered glass of the other house. He felt suddenly sick with panic. His throat rasped on the words when he called the dog. He groped his way towards the fence and felt there for the gate in the hedge. Only when he and the dog were going through did he remember how Irene Suttle's body must have dragged against the branches, but his gaze was on the house. There was no sign of life now, but when he reached the house he could see the back door was ajar and the dog growled.

Winton put his hand gently on the door and let it swing inwards. The dog snarled then, and blinding light flashed over them both.

Then Kiley's voice, high, excited, exclaimed, "My god, you scared the wits out of me!" Then he snapped, "Quieten that brute!" as the dog snarled again.

George's hand on the dog's neck silenced it. Kiley said then, on a quieter note, almost apologetically, "I keep going back. Somehow I can't believe it, even now. Mad, isn't it? Stark, raving mad, yet I can't stop it. I keep expecting her to be alive the next time I go in. Do you . . . want to look at her?"

"Good grief no!" The suggestion so startled and shocked him he stepped backwards and nearly fell over the dog's taut body. He saw, in the instant before Kiley moved back into shadow behind the torchlight, a smile, lopsided and cruel, on the other man's face, and he knew Kiley had asked the outrageous question just to turn the knife of self-hatred tighter.

George said sharply, "Annie insisted on coming, too.

When you didn't answer I was afraid something had happened to you."

"I'm sorry," Kiley spoke almost humbly. "Is she round the front? I'll go through the house and let her in. But I wish you hadn't brought her. I don't want to drag her into this."

"She insisted." He didn't add that when Annie insisted on something it was useless resisting.

Kiley moved inside his house and Winton made himself follow; made himself go through the doorway he shrank from and down the passage. He could see, out of the corner of his eye, the grey and orange checks on the linoleum floor of the kitchen as they walked past. He tried not to look, but they held his gaze in fascination.

He was glad when all three of them were in the huge lounge. Kiley went over to the glass wall and drew the golden taffeta curtains over it so that the room became suddenly warm and glowing, then in a sudden excess of hospitality that George found strangely pathetic, drawing him again from dislike to something approaching kinship with the other man, Kiley began to press drinks and food on them. Annie wanted to refuse, but with that feeling of kinship still in him, George put his hand on her own, silencing her with a quick look, while he accepted drinks and cheese and biscuits for them both, and Kiley, as he knew would be the case, never noticed that the things were left untouched.

Kiley said, when he finally settled, "I've been looking through the reports of the Griffen case. I had the office send up all we wrote about it at the time the thing broke." He leaned forward, his pale gaze flickering from one to the other. "In the Griffen case they were rung at ten minutes past three and Griffen was told to be at the railway at half past three, to place the money, in a parcel, in a locker there. And you told me you were rung shortly before half

76

past two and told to be at the surf sheds with the cash in a suitcase, at ten to three . . ."

"They said more," George reminded. "They told me to drive straight away from the place and keep driving, anywhere I chose, for half an hour before going back home."

Kiley said impatiently, "Leave that. It's not important. The other is. The point is you were both given a definite time to be there and very little time to make it in. I've gone over the routes you both must have taken. To get there you'd have had to go at high speed. That would make it easier to spot a car following you. See that point? There'd be another reason for the short time allowed, too —it was so short it would have been difficult to swing the police into action even if you got a message through.

"Listen, what I'm thinking is this. They're likely, aren't they, to stick to plans that were successful last time. A rush journey over little time and then . . . if they stick to what they did in the other cases, the place they make me head for will have lockers of some sort. I thought at first that was crazy—the locker business I mean and a fairly crowded place, but when you look at it, it's a damn sight safer than a lonely spot somewhere out the back of beyond. Listen, a man would get away much easier among a crowd, wouldn't he? And he could turn the key and remove the cash and still claim he was as innocent as Saint Peter. Did you work that out? He could say he saw a parcel put inside and the depositor forget to remove the key, so he himself just moved in for easy pickings and he knows nothing about kidnapping or anything else. See the beauty of the dodge?

"So why shouldn't they stick to the same thing this time? There's no station within a short distance of here. Nothing but the surf sheds at Warrain and that's twenty-five minutes drive from this house, if you speed and have a clear road. I doubt if they'd make it a longer trip than that. If they do—it'll be too bad, that's all."

There was sudden silence. Winton hadn't realized till then how loudly the younger man had been speaking. His ears seemed to be ringing still with the spate of words and Kiley's voice, but now other sounds faded in—the dull rumble from far out at sea, and the pinging of insects striking at the wire screen over the windows at the front of the room.

Winton felt a long chill of panic sliding down his sweating body. He thought of Annie saying that Evan Kiley was the type who would place getting even above every other thought.

He said, almost whispering, "You're going to get the police to stake the place out. You're going to . . ."

"God almighty, no!" Kiley's pale eyes were glittering, the freckles standing out lividly against his long face. "Do you think I want Robin killed? But," he reached for cigarettes, lit one, dragging on it for several seconds before he went on in a quieter voice, "But I want a sight of whoever comes for the cash. I want to be able later on to describe a face, a walk, clothes, everything possible. And I can't be there staking out the lockers at Warrain, so I've got to ask you to do it.

"Listen, it would be quite easy, wouldn't it, for you to hang round in the dressing sheds? You know what those places are—just showers, toilets, lockers, a few benches . . . there are people coming and going the whole time. No one notices anyone else. You could stay there all day, keeping the lockers in sight and . . ."

Winton shook his head. "No. You're gambling with Robin's life. They'd look the place over themselves, wouldn't they, long before they rang you to come with the money? They'd see me and recognize me and . . . it's impossible."

"You're wrong, George, quite wrong." Kiley's mood had changed. He seemed suddenly to be riding on the crest of some high-soaring excitement. He said eagerly, "In swim-trunks, you'd look different. You could sleek your hair back instead of having a side parting the way you have now. You could put on dark glasses, use some fake tan liberally over yourself. Besides, if you see someone hanging around too long you can pack up and get out, fast. You'd have to use your mother wit. You can stretch out on a bench and pretend to be sleeping; use the showers; take over one of the toilets—anything you like so long as you keep those lockers in sight."

Winton knew that his round features must be expressing the doubt he felt, and the refusal to commit himself, for Kiley's mood changed again, to a savage, "And why should they poke around beforehand, George? They won't arrive till the call to me goes through and then they'll be watching for the police, in case I played the fool at the last moment, but they won't expect me to. You're my guarantee that I'll play along. You and Annie." His gaze switched to her. His pale eyes were half slitted as he let his gaze linger on her, but she seemed to George quite unconscious of the cool impertinence of Kiley's look. She just went on sitting there, her face a mask closed to any expression, as he went on, "I've brought you into this and they know how they stand with you. They'll be expecting you, just as I said before, to make me play along, too. And," he finished flatly, "it's the one way I can see of getting a lead on them. Unless you can think of another."

"No." George looked down at his hands. He found himself dwelling on the fact that the nails looked faintly blue-tinged, as though he was cold in spite of the muggy warmth of the room. He said at last, "You're right, I suppose. It's a good plan really."

"If it works." Annie's voice was the tone George had

heard her use when she had cried in the darkness, "I'm frightened". "I wouldn't risk it. I just wouldn't care to . . ."

Kiley leaned forward and his hand, slim fingered, with a brown mole on the little finger, clasped round her bare arm. "Do you want me to do nothing so another kid could go sometime? What," his face thrust down towards hers, "What, Annie, if you have another kid and they decide that as George was such a sweet, soft touch last time, they'll take you both for another ride? Well?" He released her arm and stood back, half smiling at her.

She didn't say anything. George wondered, if like himself, the breath had been knocked out of her. He wondered too if Kiley knew, or guessed, that there would be another child in the course of six months; another child who might, as Kiley had so brutally suggested, disappear because he and Annie had remained silent and been, as Kiley had put it, such a sweet, soft touch.

He said, almost without thinking of what he was saying, "I'll do it of course. You know I'll do it."

CHAPTER EIGHT

IT was a repetition of the previous morning—the shrill ringing of a telephone bell, the sharp awakening, the groping for the phone and a mumbled "hello" as he yawned sleepily.

"It's Miriam," the voice said, then asked, "Were you awake?"

"Yes," he lied.

"I didn't realize ... not till after I'd dialled you ... what the time was."

"You've been awake all night then, haven't you?" he asked sharply.

"Yes. I couldn't possibly sleep. I'm frightened so for Robin and ... Evan won't tell me what he's going to do, and I'm terrified he'll do something mad. You don't know Evan like I do! When he gets crossed ... oh, I can't explain, but it would only take one moment's forgetting about Robin, wouldn't it? If he lost his temper, say? And then ..." her voice choked off into silence, then she thrust at him urgently, "I want to know what he's going to do. When I went back last night to ask what was happening, he was excited. I know him so well that I know that means he's planning something."

"It's all right," he broke in. "It's all right, I tell you. There won't be anything foolhardy ..." even as he went on speaking soothingly to her he was wishing he could tell her the truth; explain to her as he had done the previous night to Annie, as she had lain in his arms in the darkness; explain that he considered his agreement with Kiley's plans a guarantee that Robin would come safely back.

"If I'd refused he would have tried finding some other

way of getting a look at whoever comes," he had told her, his fingers lost in the flame-red hair. "This way, he'll leave the money and he'll go away as they tell him to and leave it to me to watch. The other way—I daren't trust to it. If he has too much to drink before he goes, or loses his temper or his head . . . I had to agree, Annie. There was no way out."

She had told him he was right. He would have liked Miriam to say the same thing, but he had promised Kiley that he'd let out no hint to Miriam of what they were doing.

"It's not spite," Kiley had said swiftly as he had demanded the promise. "It's just that I know Miriam. She panics at the drop of a hat and gets hysterical. She might turn up snooping round and lose her head . . ."

Remembering that George remembered Miriam saying she knew Kiley so well. He found himself reflecting how stupid it was that two who knew each other so well and had so much in common, should now be separated by such a gulf, even as he was remembering his own comment to Kiley, "It's a wonder you aren't afraid *I'll* do some damn silly thing—take a swing at whoever comes, for instance, remembering Vicky."

He remembered the sting of Kiley's, "But, George, that's the last thing I'd think of you doing," and the faint cruel curve of the lips that accompanied it.

"So there's nothing . . ." he became conscious of Miriam's relieved voice in his ear. "He's not going to be stupid after all. I'm glad he's not older—Robby, I mean. That he doesn't know he's a prisoner. I've always feared that, being a prisoner I mean. I can't even stand being shut up in four walls. Did you know Evan put in that glass wall just because I wanted to be able to see all the outdoors and feel I wasn't in a room at all? The room I have here has big windows too. I can see the clouds all day and at night I don't pull the curtains and there are the stars . . ." she went on talking, her voice soft, monotonously flat, till he broke in with a quick:

"Miriam, you're alone, aren't you?"

There was silence, then she said, "So you've seen through me ringing up like this? You know I just had to have someone to talk to?"

"Why don't you go back to Comboroo?"

"No! We'll only fight and here I've my work. There'll be rehearsals this morning. That will help. I'll be all right now." Her voice was lighter. "I'm sorry I rang so early. And . . . tell Annie I'm sorry we've dragged everything up again for you both. Tell her . . ."

"Miriam," he urged, "Come over here to us."

"No. I told you there are rehearsals. I'll be fine."

•   •   •

The kidnappers were following the pattern they had set in his own case.

Kiley reported that the third phone call had come, telling him to pack the money into a suitcase. The instructions, so he reported, were given swiftly, were not repeated, and to his frantic angry questions as to Robin's safety and comfort there had been only silence.

On Thursday morning George drove back to Comboroo with the money in a briefcase on the seat beside him. He had made no attempt to parcel it up because, as Kiley had demanded should be the case, there was only nineteen thousand and one hundred and fifty pounds. Kiley would have to add the remainder and parcel it as instructed.

Kiley looked tired and strained, his long chin unshaven, as he opened the door. Under his scrutiny, under the cool raking of the pale eyes, Winton felt himself reddening, but Kiley didn't make any comment at the way his visitor had been standing on the doorstep, fascinated gaze riveted on the shuttered house next door.

Kiley said at last, "Come on in," and turned away, leaving his guest to close the door and follow him into the big lounge. "Want a drink?" Kiley asked then. "If so, you'll have to settle for ginger ale. I threw the rest down the mountainside to settle the question of whether I'll be drunk or sober when the call comes. That fix your mind? Next door . . ." he paused, "had a visitor. I forgot to tell you. One of the solicitors who's trustee for the old woman's estate. It was about the rent I expect. He didn't stay long. I expect that's why she wanted the blasted cream cake. It's just the sort of thing she'd think of—to hand him a crumpled cheque with one hand and a soggy piece of cream cake with the other. She was a nasty little creature. I've had it out of Miriam that she got a fair bit of Miriam's salary for the information she doled out; for the promise to sign that statement. I suppose if I'd found out she'd have touched me for a bit more to swear herself blue in the face that Miriam was an unfit mother during the month she was here before Miriam walked out on me."

George asked suddenly, "What about her mail? There could be other appointment she made . . ."

"It isn't delivered up here. We have to go into the post office and I can't ask for hers without having questions asked. So far no one's asked about her. I don't want to lie if I can avoid it, or I might find myself stumbling over the lies, but with heaven's grace on our side this'll be over today or tomorrow. They won't keep Robin longer than they positively have to, will they?"

He looked vaguely round the room then said abruptly, "When all this is over and the mess over her death is finished I'm pulling up stakes. There's nothing to keep me here except my job and I can find better. I should have gone years ago, only I was born here; I had that land here; I was in a rut, you could say, and I couldn't see anything better than buying the paper eventually and staying here for good. Now—I just want to get out. I couldn't go on living here." The brightness was growing in his pale eyes. "Maybe Miriam and I can get together again and work something out. God knows. That, and where I'll finish up. I might even go overseas."

"I'll need your address. If the land comes good there'll have to be an adjustment made in the price I paid."

"Trying to salve your conscience with generosity?" the half-smile of cruelty was back on Kiley's face. "Save your breath. You might lose your money. You might make a killing. It won't concern me and I don't want anything from you bar what I'm taking now."

Silently George pushed the briefcase across the table between them. Kiley didn't thank him. He just nodded and said crisply, "The call might come any time now I've been told how to parcel it up, mightn't it? How about you getting along and moving into that dressing shed?"

"As you like." He wanted to stop and tell Kiley precisely why he had agreed to the plan; tell him that he thought it was the wrong thing to do but he was doing it because he feared Kiley might take worse steps. He wanted to say, "Don't blame me if this goes wrong," and unbidden, the words rose to his lips and shattered the silence.

Kiley nodded. "I won't, George. Not any more than I'm blaming you right now."

* * *

The tense excitement of the first few hours had slowly given way to a lesser excitement that had dwindled to a faint irritation, then to tiredness and finally to an exhaustion of senses that had several times sent him to the verge of sleep, only to jerk himself awake in heart-jumping panic, his frantic gaze turning again to the blank wooden faces of the lockers opposite.

85

The place was startlingly chill in spite of the warmth of the day, yet in seemingly no time his body was running with sweat. He kept looking down at his narrow chest and thin legs; kept peering at his round pale features in the only handy mirror and thinking what an absurd picture he must make moving slowly between showers and toilets, reclining on the benches, buying cigarettes at the slot machine or trying to force the other machine to disgorge the chewing gum for which he had already expended three coins without success.

He hadn't thought about food in the beginning and was surprised that in spite of the sick panic that churned in his stomach he could later grow hungry. He went out then and bought dry tasteless sandwiches in flamboyant wrappings from the beach kiosk, always with one eye alert to the entrance of the dressing sheds, but there was no sign of Kiley and finally it was time for the place to be closed for the night.

He wondered, as he backed his station waggon from the parking lot and started back towards Comboroo, if he would be missed the following day if he never turned up—if Kiley would turn from the lockers, his gaze searching for him. He knew that in all conscience and sanity he should feel, with Kiley, a desire to get even for what had been done to himself and Annie—should feel a hot rage that would make his return a keen pleasure, yet for the life of him he could feel nothing but a weary desire to get it over and be done with the whole thing. Even his talk to Annie—his expressed statement that he intended to go now to the police about Victoria's going—held no reality for him. His one need was for peace and a relaxation of the gnawing hatred of self that had torn at him for the past couple of days.

Then abruptly, so that his hands were instantly shaking and he had to halt the car, he realized that he wouldn't be out of it when he had done his part. Kiley had neatly tricked him. Perhaps unintentionally, but had tricked him just the same. He, George Winton, would be the only one who would see who came to the locker when Kiley left the money. He would be the sole person who could describe the man. He would have to give that evidence to the police; perhaps even later on in a court of law. And the police would surely remember those rumours of nine months ago when Victoria had gone. They would put two and two together and know why Kiley had gone to the Winton home and why Winton had been the one who had stayed there as a witness to whoever took the money.

So, whether Kiley had intended it or not, in spite of his promise to remain silent about Victoria, the Wintons would have to tell the whole story to the police. They would have to live through the confusion of days and nights dogged both by police and the press and every sensation-monger who swarmed to the place out of curiosity. He wondered almost idly, as he set the car moving again, how many people would condemn him and Annie for having remained silent. There would be probably anonymous letters, he reflected. And unpleasant telephone calls. All the filth spewed up by minds with nothing better to do.

He turned slowly on to the mountain road and went on up, his mind busy with plans to get Annie and Victoria out of the centre of the nightmare ahead. When he pulled up he could see the Kiley house was a blaze of lights and he wondered if the other man was pacing up and down in an agony of frustration or simply sitting there in the hope of another call that would tell him how his son was. He could remember all the bitterness of the hours of waiting when the money was ready and they waited for that last call to give them back Victoria. He tried to dwell on the bitterness, to draw some rage up into himself, but there was still only the weary desire to be done with the whole thing.

Finally he went up to the house. There was a line of light between the door and the frame—a slender thread. He put his hand on the panels of the door, wondering if Kiley had gone back to the other house as he had done the previous night, then he pushed the door wide and went on into the place. There was only silence, even when he called Kiley's name, and when he walked into the big lounge. The curtains were drawn back so that the glass wall was a sheet of darkness across the dimly lit room. Against the darkness were two figures—a man and a woman—pressed there like cut-out figures, the man's hand on the woman's arm as they half-faced each other, half-faced towards the newcomer. The man's tallness made the woman seem frailer and smaller than ever. This time she was wearing a dark blue sleeveless dress so that her body seemed almost a part of the dark glass behind her; so that her features, masked in rigidity, seemed startlingly clear.

For a moment George stood there awkwardly, wondering if he had walked in on a reconciliation, or on a quarrel. He said feebly, "Well, it didn't happen. I mean, you haven't had the call to deliver it yet."

Kiley said without moving, "Oh yes, I did. It came at four o'clock."

"But . . ." abruptly George slumped into the nearby chair and pulled out cigarettes. He felt suddenly in desperate need of a drink, realizing with astonishment that his throat must have been sore for a long time, because now it was a searing pain. He said huskily, "So you were wrong and it was a different spot."

"A motel. A motel room. I was to go there and there'd be a key in the door and I was to walk in and leave the money on the bed and walk out. I'd thought of something like that, you know," he was speaking so rapidly the words slurred and tripped each other, "but I wiped it out because it seemed too risky—a room like that has a phone, I told myself, and I could maybe risk a tip-off to the police and then I thought as lockers had been used in your case and with the Griffens . . ."

"So you were wrong," George repeated, and felt abruptly the rage and desire for revenge that he hadn't been able to feel before. Now that the ransom had been paid and the kidnappers had got away with it he felt a wild rage that they had escaped his eyes; a wild regret that now he would never be able to describe one of them.

Then he remembered the more urgent point. He asked, almost yelled at Kiley, "The boy?"

"Safe and well. He's at a farm near Clareville."

"Clare . . ." George frowned. He said, his voice wondering, stupified, "You mean you haven't checked? Been out?"

Kiley said abruptly, "Miriam, clear out of this." When she didn't move he gave her a little shove away from him. He repeated, "Clear out."

After a moment she obeyed. She didn't look at George, though she had to pass close to him to get to the door. He could see her eyes were enormous, her face deadly pale. She went without speaking and Kiley's gaze followed her till she had gone, then he said, turning his face towards the darkness of the wall, "I've something to tell you. I've no apologies to make because . . . they'd be an insult in the circumstances. I wouldn't have told you but for . . . but leave that for the moment.

"I went as I was told, to that motel room. The key was in the door, so I turned it and went in. It was the usual sort of place. You know, a single bed, chest of drawers, bit of carpet . . . but then you're in the business, so you'll know. And there was a shower off it, though I didn't notice, then. I put the cash down. I was angry, and feeling

89

a bit sick, at the way I'd been outwitted. There was a phone there, too. I didn't try to touch it. I went on out.

"And I couldn't get away. I'd parked near the office because of course I didn't know where the room was. Room number eight, the voice told me. I had to find it. And there was another car parked behind me with luggage all over the place and a man and woman and a swarm of kids hanging round. I had to wait while they shifted some of the luggage and got out of the road. I was sweating. I got into the car finally and I could see the door. Of number eight. In the rear vision mirror. And I saw a woman come running out and get into a little Morris."

"A woman?"

"Miriam."

Then he swung round. He asked savagely, "Why don't you say something, George? Why didn't you yell or say your ears have foxed you or that you think I'm off my head?" He swung back to face the glass. His voice was level again when he went on, "well it's none of those things. It was Miriam. I was out and running towards the Morris before I had time to think.

"She'd been in the shower recess, so she told me. She'd heard a car start up somewhere outside and leave and she thought that was me and it was safe to move. So she came on out.

"You see, George, there wasn't a kidnapping at all. Not what you could call kidnapping, and now we've got to throw ourselves on your mercy, because if you tell what you know Miriam's going to prison. Keep that in your head while I tell you the rest.

"Miriam wanted Robin's custody and was paying Irene to help her get it. She made a deal with Irene. Irene was going to sign a nice little document painting me redder than the devil and was going to hand Robin over to Miriam as soon as I was out of the road at a convenient moment. With Robin hidden from me and with that signed statement in her hand, Miriam was going to court to demand custody of the kid.

"Got that?

"Irene rang her Sunday; told her to come Monday night as I would definitely be out of the road. Miriam turned up as planned and then Irene suddenly developed cold feet, or apparently so. She was afraid of what I would do. Terrified of my temper. A whole heap more. Miriam could only have the kid if she tied Irene up, so I would think Irene had no part in the job.

"Listen, George, Miriam was in a panic. I told you she gets hysterical easily, didn't I? She agreed. She didn't realize till she was on her way to the farm—it belongs to her cousin Alex—that she'd put herself in an impossible position. She worked it out, and was almost certainly right, that Irene was going to tell me Robin had been taken by force and that if I liked to pay up nicely—after all I was rich, wasn't I, George?—she'd go to court and tell a beautiful story of being bound, gagged and whatever I liked. The court wouldn't look kindly on such violence, would it?

"By then it was too late, of course. Miriam decided to go ahead with her plans anyway. She left Robin with Alex and his wife and Alex rang me up—it was just coincidence he rang when my lights went on that way, George—to tell me he had Robin and would ring again the following morning. Alex was excited—he didn't give his name at first—just blurted out that they had Robin. He expected me to say something—that we'd talk. When I slammed down the receiver he thought Irene had told me everything and I wasn't going to talk to him, so he didn't even bother ringing me back again that night.

"Then I rang Miriam and told her Irene was dead. She came on out in panic. She thought at first I must have roughed Irene up in rage and killed her. She was scared out of her wits, of course. Can't you see that, George. Irene was dead. Then Miriam found *she* was responsible. She'd tied Irene up and the only person who could prove it was done at Irene's request was dead. Can you see the mess she was in? Then I dragged her to you.

"She decided to play along with the idea it was a kidnapping. She thought she could get away with it. That no one would find out the truth. And I caught her."

He turned, looking at the other man, his pale eyes blank. "It was an accident, George. If anyone was to blame it was Irene herself. Can't you understand that? And what else could Miriam do except try to save herself? Do you blame her?"

"No." He felt an insane desire to laugh. The whole thing had taken on the absurdity of a farce. In spite of himself he gave way to a gust of bellowing laughter. He leaned forward, rocking in mirth. He took off his glasses, rubbing at smarting eyes, with grunts and gurgles of laughter tearing at his raw painful throat.

Then Kiley asked solemnly, "What's so funny, George?"

George tried to point out the obvious, but laughter stifled his words, and then was instantly cut off as Kiley said, "You've forgotten Irene's really dead, haven't you? That we're in a hell of a mess."

"Dear god . . ." George's laughter was gone.

Kiley said almost absently, "I'm not an atheist. At least I don't think I am, but I've never yet known a prayer for help to be answered by a miracle. It's all left in your own hands." He held his hands up in front of him as though seeing them with new critical eyes, while George watched, his mouth slack. Then he said, letting his hands fall again, "Miriam's not going to prison, George. She's not even going to be questioned by the police and maybe blurt out something in hysteria that she can't fight down.

Listen, you were silent enough when it suited yourself about something that concerned you and Annie. You're going to be silent about this. Aren't you?" The pale eyes were hard. "You're going to go away from here and forget you ever heard of us or Irene Suttle or anything else."

"You're going to leave her in there?" He couldn't stop the revulsion creeping into his voice at the thought of the shuttered house and the slow processes of decay taking all human dignity from what had once been a woman. "Till someone eventually finds her?"

"Don't be a fool." Kiley sounded more tired than angry. "What would be the good? When the rent's no longer paid the solicitors will open the place—in the matter of a week or so I should expect. Listen, what do you think would happen then? They'd know she died from gassing. They'd think she was murdered, wouldn't they? And where does that leave us? Oh sure, they wouldn't know the truth, but there'd be questions in plenty and everyone knows she spent most of her time in here with Robin. Sooner or later Miriam would crack under it. I know that. No, don't interrupt," he waved the other man to silence. "I'm going to get rid of her. That shocks you to the depths of your staid little soul doesn't it, George?" There was mockery again in the long, freckled face. "But is it any worse than you staying silent about what happened to Victoria, so it could happen again. You don't know it hasn't really happened somewhere, now do you? There might be others like you, all yellow enough to keep their lips buttoned . . ." he rubbed one hand slowly over his face, "to hell with that. Listen, what I'm telling you is I'm going to get rid of her. It's the only thing to be done. She came here out of the blue and she can go back into the blue. I doubt if anyone here's going to miss her. She had that place on a weekly tenancy which allowed her to shoot through any time she wanted. I got that out of

Miriam. Irene told Miriam about it when she first landed here. She told her she didn't know how long she'd stay. She probably told the solicitors the same thing, so why should they bother about her doing a sudden flit? I doubt if there'll be even any talk about her—she didn't seem to chum up with anyone here. If I'm asked, I shan't know anything, except that the house's shut up and she isn't around any more. There's no better plan I can settle on. She's just got to disappear. It's not satisfactory, but tell me something that is. It's better than having her found and the police thinking it's murder, and it's better than the truth. Why should Miriam get shut up in some stinking prison for something that isn't her fault?"

George remembered the soft voice speaking of prison; of Kiley putting in the glass wall so that Miriam should feel she wasn't confined by four walls. He felt suddenly deadly tired. It was an effort to speak and the words came out in a thick, slurred voice as he asked, "You mean you're going to bury her somewhere in the scrub?"

"Lord above no! Are your trying to ram me into more trouble? A thousand things could go wrong with that— what if the scrub's suddenly cleared—have you forgotten about the new bridge opening this place up? She'd be found sooner or later. But listen, George, the sea's down there. It's hidden plenty before this and it's got to hide her. You're shocked, aren't you? You think it's indecent not to have a priest and a lot of fancy words and a wooden coffin with silver handles and some flowers to take the edge off the unpleasant fact of death, but when you're dead you're dead, George. She can't feel anything or know anything and, mean-hearted as she was, I doubt if she'd want Miriam to be sent for a prison term for what's happened. No one would want it. Except . . . a judge and a jury and maybe public opinion.

"I'm going to take her out to sea and all her things, too,

and leave her. It's the only way. Or can you think of some other way out?"

After a long time Kiley said flatly, "You can't. I'll get a boat tomorrow—hire it for twenty-four hours or longer. If there's another storm I might have to wait, and I can't work in daylight. When I have the boat and it's calm I'll put her in the car and take her down to the boat and out to sea ... so go home. Tell Annie however much you think's necessary and then forget us and this and everything else."

He came forward softly to stand just in front of the elder man. "Are you going to do it?"

George said slowly, not answering the question, "You told me you had trouble carrying her next door. How're you going to manage getting her aboard a boat without making a hash of the job?"

The pale eyes seemed to film slightly. Kiley turned away, reaching for another cigarette. Blowing out a cloud of smoke he said, "When you've got to do something you can wangle it some way, and the other night I was shocked sick at the idea she was dead before I started in moving her."

"You'll never manage it." George shook his head. "You wouldn't be able to leave the boat out from some beach and put her in a dinghy and take her out that way—you'd upset the dinghy trying to get her aboard. You'll have to tie up at a jetty or marina somewhere and you can't struggle along that with a burden like ... like that. Those places aren't quiet at night—there are too many men go night-fishing for a start, and sometimes there are boats being repaired or painted under floodlights. No, I'm not carping for the sake of it. I know it for a fact. I've a boat of my own ..."

He saw Kiley turn, saw the narrowing of the pale eyes and his stomach muscles seemed to clench into a hard knot of revulsion even as he said quite evenly, "The best thing

95

is for me to help you and to use my boat. That way there won't be any need to hire one and you'll have help. We can use my station waggon. I often drive down to the marina for night-fishing. No one will comment on seeing it parked down there."

"It's your suggestion. I didn't ask you." The words were grudging, ungracious, but George ignored them. He knew that if their positions were reversed he would feel the same—for the past three days Kiley had lived with hatred for what he had thought the Wintons' crime of silence. Now his wife was the criminal and he had to be beholden to the very man he had called a stinking coward. He wondered what Kiley was thinking as the tall figure went on standing there, motionless, not even drawing now on the cigarette that was clasped in his left hand.

Then abruptly he turned. He said, "All right, if you want it that way, let's get it over. It's calm tonight. There might be storm again tomorrow. And the day after. And the one after that." There was suddenly a white line round his mouth. "The sooner it's over . . . can you get your boat out tonight?"

"Yes. What about her things?"

"They'll have to be packed. She has suitcases somewhere. I remember the day she came Miriam snooped from behind the curtains—I guess Annie's done the same on new neighbours sometimes."

Surprisingly George found himself smiling. He saw that Kiley had relaxed too. Kiley said lightly, "A little light relief eh, George. By all means keep our sense of humour." Then abruptly he folded up into the cushioned depths of the blue chair beside him, bending his head over so that it rested on tight clenched hands on his knees. He stayed like that for several seconds, then slowly lifted his head. There were tears in the pale eyes and George felt a shrinking revulsion of embarrassment.

He said, too loudly, "Would you know her things from those belonging to the house?"

Kiley blinked dazedly. He answered slowly, "Well, I guess hers would be clothes, wouldn't they? I doubt if she had much else. She brought two cases and a smallish trunk. A dog box, Miriam called it, I remember. That reminds me, listen, what'd you do with the blasted cat?"

"Found it a home. We'll have to use our judgment, that's all. Would . . . is Miriam going to be all right here on her own?"

"She'll have to be, that's all. Where's this marina you've been talking about?"

"Below Coorong."

"Will it be quiet there yet?"

"Hard to tell. There could be people out night-fishing—maybe someone working on the boats."

"They likely to be curious if they see you lugging stuff aboard?"

"If they've time to kill they'd come over for a yarn, offer help, ask was I planning a trip—that sort of thing." He sat fingering his glasses with sweating hands, rubbing over the lenses with his handkerchief as he said, "I should have thought this out before. There'll be the caretaker around no matter what time we turn up. If we leave it till everyone's likely to be in for the night or well out to sea till daylight, he'll wonder why we're taking stuff aboard so late. He'll probably hang round talking and watching. The best thing would be to turn up just before dawn. We could be heading out for a day's fishing. He won't be curious, and if there's anyone else about, they'll be heading out themselves and too busy to be concerned with us."

"Makes sense," Kiley spoke grudgingly as though he was actively resenting the older man's efforts to help. He asked, "What do we do in the interval? Pack up her things now and . . . I'd vote for trying to rest. Shut your mind on it all you like, it's still going to be hell, isn't it? And the later we leave moving her things out the less likely it is someone will turn up and see us around. Right?"

CHAPTER NINE

HE didn't sleep and he knew the Kileys didn't, because in the silence of the house he could hear them whispering on and on till the sound was an irritation and he felt an urgent desire to go and knock on the wall dividing the spare room from theirs. Miriam Kiley had gone to her room as though by right, as though her parting and desertion of her husband had never happened at all. Lying awake smoking, blinking at the square of window where two stars showed, George thought of the Kiley marriage and the future and himself and Annie; particularly of Annie and what she would say when he told her what he had done.

She would hate it, of course. That was a foregone conclusion but like himself she would know he could have done nothing else. Neither he nor Kiley wanted their part in it, but the alternative was to send Miriam to prison and none of it, neither inquest, nor trial, nor judge or jury, could give life back to Irene Suttle.

When Kiley came softly into the room at last, George switched on the light. He swung his stockinged feet to the floor and said shortly, "All right. I'll be there in a minute," and reached for his shoes, fumbling in an urgent haste now to be done with the whole job.

He had thought that the packing of her things would be the easiest part of what lay ahead. Instead it proved the worst, because it brought vividly alive to him the woman that Kiley had described as slightly grubby, blonde and lonely. There were long fair hairs caught in the hair brush with its chipped pink enamel back; there were dresses, shapeless and tasteless for the most part, hanging in the closet, some with the faintly stale smell of too long wearing

99

about them; one with a torn and drooping hem; a grubby underskirt balled and pushed into a corner of one of the drawers, as though long forgotten by the owner, and a coat, too heavy for the hot hard sunshine of the coast, in loud green and yellow checks, on which the dead woman had at some time tacked a collar of some thick brown fur.

Even her shoes, old fashioned in their thick heels and stubby toes, helped bring her to life there at his elbow while he and Kiley sweated over folding and thrusting her things into the trunk and the two suitcases.

She came alive to him in the few books that were inscribed on the flyleaf with her name in thin upright writing. They were romances for the most part, well thumbed, and carefully covered in plastic, as though she had read them over and over, losing herself in their printed dreams. He found them strangely pathetic; found himself with a feeling of guilt as though he had crudely invaded the last shreds of her privacy.

The sight of her blanketed body there on the bed, and even the sweetish smell of death that hung over the room touched him far less. It was as though his mind had accepted the horror of death and had come to a certain point of disgust and revulsion and could go no further there and was now only alive to the cold stripping of privacy and dignity.

There was only one photo—of an elderly woman. In a black frame, and obviously enlarged from some snapshot, it stood on the bedside table. He found it heart-wrenching and pitiful that the only thing to share her room had been memories of a dead woman.

He wanted to talk to Kiley about it, but looking at the tight-lipped, freckled face with the beads of sweat on the upper lip, he felt that Kiley would neither understand or want to talk. He was only intent on getting rid of the last vestiges of unpleasantness. He wondered suddenly how

Kiley, who had once said he couldn't have lived, as Winton had done, in silence about a crime, was going to live with this. And more important, how Miriam Kiley was going to live with it.

He was shivering, in spite of the heat, when they loaded the cases into the back of the station waggon and turned back to the house. He felt his dislike against his companion rearing up again when Kiley said, his voice soft with relief, "We just have to shift her now and then we can get off."

Winton stopped dead. The darkness wasn't complete in spite of the moonless night. The stars were too bright for that. Winton looked up at them as he said, "To you she's nothing more than a nuisance, to be disposed of as quickly as possible. Isn't she?"

Kiley had been heading up the steps to the house again. He swung round, the starlight just pricking up the lines of his features. He said, his voice tired, "If I wallow in sentimentality I'm going to crack. I'm warning you, George. I'll crack. I don't want to think about her or what you and I are doing. I just can't afford to. All I'm going to think about is keeping Miriam clear of trouble." He swung round again, his back to Winton as he marched into the house.

George followed more slowly. He was dawdling deliberately and knew it. He didn't want to take part in the final effacing of Irene Suttle from her home. He stood there in the little porch and noticed then that there was a draggled square of white paper on the verandah post. He peered at it and saw that at some time the words "No Milk" had been roughly scrawled on to it and that the scrawl had run and spread into purple streaks across the whiteness when the storm had finally broken the previous night and drenched the coast. Because he was putting off the moment of having to go inside he tore the shredded paper down, crumpling it into his jacket pocket. He tore instead a page from his little pocket diary, wrote on it neatly "No milk" and fixed it back to the pin-tack.

He looked up then to see Kiley's pale face staring at him. The younger man asked, "What the devil are you up to? Do you want some nosy neighbour to see us hanging around and ask what the devil we're doing? For god's sake get a move on."

Winton shrugged. There was no revulsion in him when he helped lift the woman's body, Kiley at the head and himself at the foot. There was only pity and a moment of searing shock because he had expected her to be rigid. Somewhere in the past somewhere he had read a phrase about the rigidity of death, and as his hands clasped and lifted, it sprung to mind and then there was no rigidity at all. He stood there, shocked, till Kiley asked urgently, "What's wrong?"

He shook his head wordlessly, backing out of the room, realizing that rigidity had passed off. He was glad he was the one to back out of the house. It meant he could look back over his shoulder and not have Kiley secretly smiling at the cowardice of averted gaze.

It was surprisingly difficult to get her on to the back seat, but finally it was done and again his dislike of Kiley flared when the younger man stood grabbling at a cigarette pack, and said almost lightly, "No breaking the speed limit, George. We'd look pretty if we got pulled up tonight. Here," he held out the crumpled packet.

George shook his head, sliding behind the wheel as he asked, "What would you say if we were?"

"Anything, George." The faint hint of mockery was in Kiley's voice. "Anything at all. That I gassed her. That you did. Anything except mention Miriam." As he met the other man's gaze he asked quickly, "Wouldn't you lie, too, if Annie was involved? If this was you and Annie instead of me and Miriam? You'd throw me overboard all right,

George, as easily as we're going to put *her* over." Then he shrugged, "I'm on edge. I'm not trying to rile you. Forget it. Just forget it."

. . .

There was no sign of anyone about when George used his key to unlock the gates leading down to the marina's jetty. He slid behind the wheel again and sat motionless, till Kiley said edgily, "What's the matter?"

"I was just wondering where the caretaker is. Somewhere in the boatsheds I expect." He nodded to the little room at the side of the gates. The door was open and there was a dim light shining inside, but no one appeared. "Not that it matters." He drove through, closed the gates again, then continued down to the boatsheds, parking the car there in the shadows, near the top of the long finger of dark jetty that pointed out into the water.

"Where's your boat?" Kiley asked softly.

"About half way down. She's the *Heron*. White, blue trim." He switched off the car lights, then added, "You'd better wait a bit till your eyes get used to the dark." They sat motionless, silent, till George spoke again, breathlessly as though all that time of stillness his breath had been held, "Now . . ." he slid out. "I think we'd better take her first. Get her on board. In case someone comes along."

"How do we see?" Kiley still sat there, his face a pale glimmer in shadow.

"I'll guide. You follow. We won't have a free hand for a torch anyway," George reminded bluntly.

Kiley expelled his breath explosively as though he, too, had been holding a pent-up breath of fear. "Right then." Now he was frantic in urgency as he flung open the rear door, "Get a move on you, damn you!" he flung across the space between them.

George didn't answer or protest. Between them they got

the blanketed body out on to the ground then, straining, lifted it between them and began to move on to the wooden planks of the jetty. To George it seemed that the night became suddenly alive with noise. He had never before realized that booted footsteps rang out on the boards with such shocking clarity. He missed a step from shock and almost stumbled, then realized that of course whenever he had stepped on to the wooden planks before, he had worn cork soles or sandshoes. For a minute dismay held him, while Kiley went on moving, so that the foot of the blanketed body suddenly pressed against his own living body. He gasped, stepping backwards and the night was a crescendo of sound again, so that he began a stumbling shuffle of frantic haste.

"My god!" Kiley breathed softly as at last the body was on deck and the two of them were standing, slack-armed, gasping, beside it, "My god, what a filthy racket!"

"We should have worn sandshoes. I forgot that. We'd be wearing them if we were going out fishing."

"You mean," Kiley sounded disgusted, "*You* should have. I am. You sounded like . . ."

He had been standing behind the older man. As the sudden burst of white light flooded over them, he gave a shrill neighing cry, throwing up one arm, stumbling backwards. George was left there, framed in stark brilliance, along with the *Heron* and the rest of the boats and the whole strip of the marina's jetty. It was only then he remember that usually three dim lights shone all night over the boats. The place shouldn't have been unlighted as it had been. Now he realized that the floodlights had been thrown so that the place was a blaze of light. He stood there, blinded, his eyes watering, while a voice, thin and nasal, shrilled out to him, "That you, Mr. Winton?"

He couldn't answer. His throat was choked tight with sheer panic. He knew the long blanketed form must be clearly visible in that searing light. He wondered how far away the caretaker was. Only when he heard the sound of sneakers coming along the jetty planks did he manage, "Yes, it's Winton."

"I give you a scare?" The steps stopped. "Hey, you see anyone around when you drove in, hmm?"

"No. Why?" His eyes had stopped watering and he could see the caretaker now—a thin figure in blue jeans and an outsize khaki sweater, both bleached to paleness in the white light.

"Been someone pussying around. I haven't just got the heebies either. Found their boat. So they're either on land or on one of the boats down there. I was listening— thought he'd come out when your car drove in. I was just going to throw the lights and nail'm when y'must've scared the bugger off. Hey, you going out?"

"For a trial run." He hesitated, searching for words to deal with any curiosity about the long bundle on the deck planks. "We'll probably cruise out over the weekend. I'm just loading a few things."

"Probably lose'm if you load now. Those buggers'd pinch your nail filings."

"There's nothing valuable." It was an effort to keep his voice apparently unconcerned; to stand still and not move; to try and hide the still form on the deck.

The other man stood hesitating, then said at last, reluctantly, "Guess I'd better move on round the sheds. You see anyone, you yell, hmm?"

"Yes."

George abruptly realized that his clothes were sticking to him; that he was running with cold sweat. And he was trembling. Only when Kiley spoke softly from behind him was he capable of moving again.

"What was all that?" Kiley asked.

"There's been someone around. Probably a couple of

105

boys out for a thrill. They come in in rowboats," it was suddenly a relief to talk, "and swarm aboard the launches; break into the cabins, pinch whatever they can put their hands on. Someone's come that way tonight and the caretaker has the boat, so whoever came is stranded on one of the boats or hanging round the sheds somewhere. The lights were off. The caretaker was hoping to fool him into coming out and trying for the gates, then when he heard someone moving he'd have thrown the floodlights and pinned him, blinded him with the lights . . ."

"Are you going to stand there babbling half the night?" Kiley broke in tightly. "Listen, you'd best go back for the cases on your own. If he sees me moving round he's likely to take me for a trouble maker and use that shotgun he was holding. I'll stay on deck."

George didn't answer. He unlocked the cabin and went in, sliding his feet out of his shoes and slipped into the stained, battered sandshoes he kept on board. He had no desire to have his every trip up and down the jetty heard and noted and commented on; with the caretaker wondering why a man going out to sea was wearing leather-soled shoes for the job.

He went without speaking, pausing half way along the still brilliantly lit jetty to light a cigarette and draw on it in slow luxury, before going back to the station waggon. The rear doors were still open and the tailboard was down. For a moment he didn't notice the oddity of the latter fact, then he was suddenly furiously angry. He turned towards the caretaker's shed before he had reflected on the unwisdom of picking a quarrel right then; of asking why the man had been curious enough to open the back of the waggon to see what was inside.

But the man's sallow face held no guilt as he turned from the stirring of instant coffee into hot water. He said grumblingly, "Blasted gate was open when I come back.

Must've slipped through while I was yacking to you. That's the fourth time in the las' fortnight. You want'ny help getting your stuff aboard?"

"No thanks. Did you open the tailboard of the waggon by any chance?" He was feeling suddenly sick, and wondered if the other man could see the way his hand was shaking in panic.

"Me? Whaffor? Hey, you mean something's gone?"

"No. No, it doesn't matter. It was open, that's all."

The other man went back to his coffee mixing. "Must've scared him off just when he was going to strip you, eh? S'long's nothing's gone . . ."

"No, no it's alright I tell you." He knew his voice was shrill and impatient, and that the other man was staring after him as he hurried out. He was almost afraid to go back to the waggon; afraid to look inside.

The small trunk was still there, jammed against the back of the rear seat, and so was one of the cases, but the second case was gone. He stood there trying to think what they had packed into it, but he couldn't remember.

He got the trunk out, hoisting it to one shoulder, grunting a little with effort as he started down the jetty again. Kiley was waiting and helped him aboard with it. Then George told him of the second case. Kiley didn't say anything for a long moment. Then he lifted his shoulders in a brief shrug. "It hardly matters. There wasn't anything worthwhile. He'll probably dump the lot somewhere. Just a case of *us* having less to dump, that's all."

"I . . . expect you're right."

"God, you're sweating, aren't you?" The cruel curve of amusement was back on Kiley's face.

George turned abruptly away. He said shortly, "Stow the trunk so it won't shift when we move out. I'll come back with the rest."

The caretaker was beside the waggon when he got back.

George could smell the coffee on the man's breath as he leaned close over George's shoulder, asking, "Sure nothing's gone, Mr. Winton?"

"Nothing."

"I've rung the police. Told them about that chap. They're coming for the boat. Ought to be here any minute." George continued bending over the case in the waggon's back. He didn't dare look round and the man pressed, "If anythin's gone . . ."

George straightened slowly. "I've told you nothing has. Keep an eye on the waggon will you? I'll be back at dawn probably."

It was an effort not to break into panic stricken running; not to jump furiously on deck and rage at Kiley to get the engine running and them moving out to sea. When he finally made the *Heron*, he said thickly, "Stow the case while I get the engine running. The police are on the way. That fool rang them—they might come down here searching in case there were two men about."

Kiley didn't say anything. He stood tight-lipped while the *Heron* slowly slid out of her berth. As they began to move out through the clutter of small boats that were moored close to the marina's shelter they could hear the police car coming along the road.

Kiley's hand was hard and warm and congratulatory on the elder man's shoulder. "We did it. Stop sweating, George. Half an hour and we can forget the whole thing."

George, heading the boat out to sea, wondered if Kiley really believed that. For himself he was certain there would never be any forgetting, yet six weeks later he had managed to push Irene Suttle and her affairs so far into the background of thought that the shock, when it came, was all the greater.

CHAPTER TEN

GEORGE had wondered afterwards if it had been Annie's pregnancy that had helped her and forced on her a remote serenity that had cushioned her against the shock of what he had told her. She had been still in bed when he had come home and had responded to his touch and voice with a sleepy murmur. When he had rung her the previous night to tell her he was staying at Kiley's she had said only, "I'm glad. He oughtn't to be alone," and he hadn't mentioned Miriam being there in the other bedroom with Kiley, or anything about the future hours.

That morning he had told her everything — of slipping out to sea in the faint waking of dawn, with Kiley's hand a hard chunk of warmth on his shoulder. He had told her bluntly of sliding Irene Suttle's blanketed body into the luminous grey of the sea under the dawn sky and of the way Kiley had straightened his tall body and said, "That's over. It's finished," as though he were capable of instant forgetfulness.

He had told her of the almost cruel beauty of the dawn over the sea, with it springing to life from grey to blue to blue-green and sapphire under a sky streaked with orange and rose pink, and their tying up of the *Heron*.

She had pulled him down tightly beside her then, as though she wanted to make her body a refuge against memory for him, while her voice, strangely remote, had whispered, her breath fluttering against his cheek, "It was all you could do, George love. The only thing."

"I keep feeling there should have been some other way out," he had told her.

"I know. It's all kind of unreal, isn't it?" They had gone

on talking in whispers for a long time; whispers that reminded him of Kiley and Miriam whispering together through the dark hours.

Finally he had told her of the abrupt parting from Kiley when the two men had gone back to the station waggon and without thinking of what he was doing George had turned it towards the road to Comboroo and then, where the road stretched grey-white ahead into blue-hazed distance, Kiley had told him to pull up. He had said, opening the car door and stepping out, "I'll hitch a ride. Listen, George, we've nothing in common and this is going to be goodbye. No, don't protest. If you're honest with yourself and with me, you'll admit you want it this way, too."

George had been held silent by a complete revulsion that he was certain was being shared by Kiley. Both of them, he was sure, were in that moment hating the other, yet in spite of it he had wanted to say something to smooth out the bitterness. But Kiley had given him no time. He had turned away, a tall figure in crumpled khaki shorts and shirt, and grubby sandshoes, hatless under the hard early sunshine and had begun to walk rapidly along the road towards Comboroo. Only when he was a tiny figure in the blue haze of distance did he halt. Winton had stayed there watching till the little figure had been finally drawn into a passing car.

The only reminder of the Kileys after that had been the lawyer's notification that the transfer of the Comboroo land was finalized. George had taken the letter to Annie, upbraiding himself for not having remembered that aspect of things, for not having offered Kiley the re-transfer of the land or an amendment of the price.

He had known, when he had taken the letter to her to where she had been sitting sewing beside the pool, watching Victoria splashing, that he was throwing onto her shoulders the burden of decision as to whether he should again get in touch with Kiley, to discuss the matter. Annie had known it, too.

"You want me to say what to do, don't you?" she had asked, her dark blue eyes again holding the remote serene look that seemed as though she were deliberately closing thought on the past. "I'd say leave it. When the whole thing — all this bridge and what-not business is finished, you can pay him a fair price then. You don't know yet how it's going to work itself out. If he wants it otherwise, he knows where you are. Anyway, he must've got one of those letter from his legal man too, mustn't he? If he wants things different he can get in touch with you, love." Then she had asked, "What do you mean to do about telling about Vicky?"

He had deliberately avoided mentioning that subject. He hadn't wanted to admit to her that he didn't want to have to face up to the police and to the publicity that would follow; that he wanted only obscurity and peace of mind, but now he answered slowly, "I can't see the point of telling now that Kiley's case wasn't . . ."

She broke in, "I know. Let's leave it, and the land business, too. You can always get in touch later on."

But when George, six weeks after Irene Suttle's death, tried to contact Kiley, he failed.

CHAPTER ELEVEN

IT was the season of swimming-pool parties and beach picnics through the long warm evenings, or, as Annie put it with wry humour, "fruit picking season", because with most of the homes empty through the evenings the sweet profitable fruits of jewellery and money were left about for easy picking.

George wasn't alarmed that Saturday morning. There was only vague irritation that his lazy floating on the air bed in the pool should be broken into, when Mrs. Gage came down to him and Annie, to say there was a policeman in the house.

"Fruit picking season." Annie shook her head at him, half smiling.

He splashed lazily to the side of the pool, called to the housekeeper to say he would be there as soon as he'd dried off, and then paused for a long appreciative look at Annie. She was impossible and she was beautiful and she was all his. Sometimes the pleasure of the fact was so great it was sheer pain to him. She was wearing a shift dress of bright orange with huge blue flowers panelling it, that should have been a complete disaster with the flame-red of her hair, yet wasn't. He wondered suddenly what outsiders must think of them seeing them together—himself round-faced and solemn and spectacled, narrow-shouldered and ordinary, and Annie so flamboyant and beautiful.

He was still thinking of that when he padded, bare-footed, into the house. After the harsh sunshine outside the place seemed dark. He couldn't see colours properly and the face of the uniformed man who stood up to greet him was only a blur. It was only later that it became a square frame to a big nose and mouth and loose-lidded sleepy grey eyes under greying brows.

There had never been an occasion when the Wintons had sought the help of the local police. When Victoria had gone, and afterwards, they had deliberately avoided the law and all its aspects. Occasionally George had seen various members of the force, on traffic duty, near the boating marina and by the beach, and more recently there had been police visiting nearby in homes that had been broken open.

He said half apologetically, "I'm afraid I don't know your name?"

"Englebert, Mr. Winton. Sergeant Bill." The voice was pleasant, the smile even more so.

Winton waved him to a chair, took another opposite, offered cigarettes and sat back expectantly, cupping his hands round the flame lighting his own cigarette. He didn't look up for a moment, till the cigarette was alight and the match flicked out, though Englebert had asked, "Have you seen this before, Mr. Winton?"

His gaze moved lazily, became fixed and rigid. He knew that the blazing shock must be visible in his face. He stared and went on staring at chipped pink enamel.

"And these, Mr. Winton?" There were two books, plastic covered, in front of him. He stared silently as the policeman produced the hand mirror that went with the hair brush and finally a suitcase—brown leather with one corner scuffed.

After that first shock George somehow found calmness. He shook his head doubtfully, then more firmly. He pretended, not knowing how far he was succeeding, to be interested and curious, but nothing more.

Englebert asked at last, "You've never seen them, Mr. Winton? That positive?"

"Should I have? The case is the cheap sort I might

have seen any place; the books ditto. I don't think I've seen the other things. Why?"

"Because we've had a report they were stolen from your station waggon at the marina on the night of the sixteenth and seventeenth of last month."

George shook his head silently.

"You were there, weren't you, Mr. Winton?"

"I couldn't tell you offhand. I'm down there a lot, but I'm damned if I could tell you the dates. Why?"

Englebert seemed at a loss. He picked up the mirror, fingering it, turning it over and over, looking at his own reflection in the glass while George felt his nerves tightening in panic as to what was coming next. Finally the other man put the mirror down. He was rubbing thoughtfully down the length of his big nose when he said, "Jacobs said you were there. He told you someone had come in in a dinghy and was hanging around somewhere."

"Jacobs? Oh you mean the caretaker? Funnily enough I've never known his name." George knew in despair that he was babbling, but he was quite incapable of stopping the flow of words. "Yes, if that was the sixteenth I was down there. Just before dawn it was, so I expect that would make it the seventeenth, would it, and Jacobs suddenly threw the master switch and near blinded me with the floodlights, then told me there was someone about and he'd sent for the police. I meant to ask if anyone had been caught, when I came on in again, but he wasn't around and I forgot all about it."

"Is that so?" Englebert spoke weightily into the sudden silence, then half apologetically he went on, "We picked up a chap at the marina night before last. When we searched his lodgings we came on this stuff, among a pile of others. He was open enough about things and claimed these were taken from a station waggon early morning of the seventeenth. He was positive of the date because it was the night he was nearly caught and lost his boat. Jacobs gave us the date and told us yours was the only station waggon there then."

George shook his head ponderously. "What am I expected to say to that? I suppose this man's speaking the truth so far as .he remembers, but they didn't come out of my station waggon. He's mixed himself up somewhere."

"You didn't lose anything that 'night? That positive?"

George hesitated for a bare fraction of a second. He had been going to give a denial, only to realize the pitfall that would lay for him. There would be no reason for a thief to claim he had stolen from one spot if he had never done so at all. It wasn't reasonable, nor feasible. He remembered, too, the way he had given the excited, almost hysterical denial of theft, to Jacobs.

"I didn't say that." He spoke sharply. "A small box of stores was taken. Nothing important. I was going to blow my top to Jacobs, then he told me the gates had been opened and the man must have cleared out and the police were coming. I cooled down then. I wanted to get out to sea, not stand around for half a day answering a lot of questions." He stopped, blinked in sudden embarrassment and added awkwardly, "That sounds ungracious and damnedably impolite. I apologize."

Englebert was smiling. "No need. You get any fish that morning, sir?"

"No." He remembered suddenly that long shape starkly silhouetted on the *Heron's* deck, and the clatter of his leather shoe soles on the jetty planks. He said quickly, "As it happens I wasn't going fishing. I was taking a lot of rubbish out to dump at sea—old carpeting, stuff like that. We'd had it hanging around for a long time."

Englebert looked up. He had for an instant, to George's gaze, the look of an alert and intelligent terrier. "Rubbish?

You wouldn't have helped out a friend, now—disposing of theirs into the . . ."

"No." The answer was out before he had thought an agreement might have been better. He sat there chewing the question and answer over anxiously then said, "I suppose you want to know the owner of that . . ." he nodded to the case, "and the other things. But they're surely not worth troubling . . ."

Englebert shook his head. "It's the name, you see." He flicked open one of the books and Winton was staring again at the thin upright writing, at the name Irene Suttle, inscribed on the flyleaf. He wondered what his face was showing, if anything, as he went on staring. "There's a call out to trace a woman of this name. We thought if the things came out of your waggon you'd mayhap know . . ."

George shook his head. Went on shaking it long after it would have been sensible to stop, while his heart was thudding in panic stricken jerks against his chest. "A call out . . ." "a woman of this name . . ." the words were clarion like in thought.

He asked at last, thickly, "What's she done? This woman you want?"

Englebert looked faintly shocked. "Now, sir, I didn't say that, did I?" he protested. "Lady's done nothing, except she witnessed an accident a while back, and a man's since died. Still there's no point troubling you with all that." He gave a last look at the mirror, placing it with the brush inside the cheap suitcase. "As you can't help . . . I expect," he gave a sudden broad grin, "the right of it is the silly fool's done so much thieving he couldn't tell his own mum where the stuff in his lodgings came from in the first place. I've seen some bower birds in my time, but never the likes of this beauty—everything from a needle to an anchor, if you'll believe me. Must be mad t've kept half of it."

George was looking out the window. He could see Annie by the pool, talking to the children. He said, half absently, "A witness would surely have given her evidence at the time of the accident, wouldn't she?"

"Right you are, but a man's died. Case of an inquest now. Probably trial, too. Case of culpable driving, if you see, Mr. Winton, but off she's hopped somewhere and there seems no tracing her. Then I came across that name," he tapped the now closed case.

"You mean," he couldn't keep the note of sharpness out of his voice, "that there's going to be a search for her?"

He wondered anxiously how it sounded to the other's ears, but Englebert only repeated, "Case of an inquest, Mr. Winton."

He was moving towards the door, obviously eager to be gone. George remained still, hearing the heavy footed tread on the carpet, seeing the plodding walk that covered the distance with surprising quickness. He wanted to shout out that he had to know what the police were doing and intended to do, but his tongue seemed suddenly swollen monstrously in his mouth. He barely nodded when Englebert turned back at the door, at the last moment, and bade him a pleasant goodbye.

He could hear the policeman and Mrs. Gage saying something to each other in the hall. He knew then an urgent desire to be with Annie, to tell her what had happened, to beg, like a frightened child, for reassurance. It was the very knowledge that his instinctive need of her was the need of comfort alone that sobered him. Instead of going out to her he went to the phone. It took him a long fretting time before Kiley's number answered, and then the voice was a stranger's.

"Kiley?" It was a thin voice, edged with impatience. "No longer here. They've moved. Sold out. No, I dunno where they are. Why ought I?"

George didn't reply. He was conscious only later of the enormity of bad manner that had let him simply slide the receiver into place without another word. His thoughts were concentrated on the fact that he had expected Evan Kiley to be able to tell him what questions the police had asked round Comboroo and what they intended doing in an effort to find the missing woman, and on the other fact that he should have realized that the Kileys would clear out of the district as quickly as possible. Hadn't Evan said that he wanted only to be rid of the house and its memories? And wouldn't Miriam Kiley have felt that in even greater measure?

But he had a horrible feeling of aloneness, of desertion, as he went out into the garden. He saw Annie turning towards him, saw the smile that started on her wide mouth and touched her eyes and welcomed him. He went to her, sitting down beside her, curving his arm over her body and she rubbed the closed knuckles of one hand gently against his cheek, asking, "What was it, love?"

The panic was still there, thumping against his ribs, when he answered lightly, "Fruit picking trouble, Annie. Just some trifles they found in a thieving bower bird's nest—that's how the policeman put it—and thought I might be able to identify. Just fruit picking season trouble—don't worry your red head over it."

•   •   •

He hadn't honestly expected Englebert to return to the house. There had been a gnawing fear in his mind that the police *might* come again, with questions about that night and the station waggon and the book with Irene Suttle's name, if the thief, whoever he was, stuck to his story about the theft, and if the police were determined to find Irene Suttle, but there had been a big element of hope in the see-saw of his thoughts that had weighted the balance in favour of him never hearing more of the matter.

But Englebert came back the next morning.

He was as polite, as affable, as good-natured as before. He was even a little apologetic, when he stood facing George that Sunday morning and said, "Thought I'd try to see you now, sir, in case you wanted to get to the eleven o'clock service."

"I'm afraid I'm not a churchgoer," George began, then stopped, hearing the note of apology, and more, in his voice. He sounded, he thought unhappily, like someone who found it necessary to appease the other man, because of a gnawing conscience. He wondered uneasily if he was merely imagining it or whether Englebert could read that apology and appeasement into the words, too.

But Englebert made no comment on the statement. He cleared his throat and looked, with blank eyes, at the abstract painting on the opposite wall. Unwittingly, George found his own gaze straying to it, puzzling over the confusion of form and colouring, till he suddenly blurted out, hearing again the tone of appeasement and apology, "That's a ridiculous thing, you know, and I don't know why I ever bought it in the first place, but it gets you after a while and somehow it seems to suit the room and of course . . ." his voice trailed off.

"I believe it's very popular."

The words were heavy, a little dubious and George was suddenly sure that Englebert would never give house-room to such a painting. He had a fleeting soaring of imagination that pictured Englebert, in shirt-sleeves and battered shorts, at ease, with his feet up in a room of conventional two chairs and settee suite of tapestry and fumed oak, with what Englebert would describe as a "nice view" in a white frame on one wallpapered wall. The picture was so vivid he felt his mouth relaxing in a smile, and then he abruptly remembered the way Kiley talked; how he had described a mental picture of Irene Suttle hurrying through the storm with Robin in her arms; how he had made Annie see Irene answering the door to a stranger, and being forced backwards . . .

He asked huskily, "Any news about this Irene Suttle?" and then, because he was afraid the other man would note how he had remembered the name, he blurted out, "Unusual name. It stuck in my mind and . . . you said you couldn't trace her."

"No, Mr. Winton, we can't."

Englebert cleared his throat again. It was an irritating sound. George found himself being unreasonably annoyed about it. About that, and the man's slowness in coming to the point of his visit.

He asked sharply, "What did you want to see me about?"

Englebert looked relieved, as though he had been waiting for his host to come to the point, too. He said almost briskly, "I was going over the question of those books with the chap concerned. Trying to find, if you follow me, if he couldn't suggest some other place he came across them. But no," he shook his greying head. "He was dead certain they were out of your waggon. He said there was another case and a smallish trunk sort of affair. That right?"

George caught himself up on the verge of lying. He remembered that Jacobs might have seen him carrying the other things to the boat.

"Yes, he's right there," he gave agreement. "One case, a box something between a trunk and a large case and a box of stores. Your man took the box of stores."

"A second case, so he says."

"And I say a box of stores." He knew his voice was too loud, almost excited. Slowly, trying to calm himself, he removed his glasses and began cleaning the lenses with painstaking care and was suddenly, in memory, doing just that in Kiley's house and wondering why the handkerchief he was using was so dirty, and thinking of Victoria ... he wondered in sudden panic if everything was going to conspire to bring back to thought what he had hoped was beginning to fade from the forefront of memory.

Englebert was gazing at the painting again, his square, suntanned face quite blank of expression. He said abruptly, "I'll tell you why he's so dead sure he's right. He knows you, you see, Mr. Winton. Knows you and your boat and your waggon into the bargain. He heard you and Jacobs talking—you saying you were loading a few things aboard. That made him look for your car. Didn't want to leave empty handed from his night's labours, as you might say." He gave a rumble of laughter deep down in his throat, but uncannily the suntanned face was still quite blank. "Saw it, and saw it was yours from the number. He said there was plenty of light by then, from the floodlights. He opened the back, took a dekko, sneaked a case and opened the gates. Those gates," he added in ponderous censure, "ought to have a good lock—not the sort of one a key turns from outside and you just turn a bit of knob from inside. If it'd been a good lock our chap wouldn't have got out that night. Now would he?"

George stared back silently. His mind was a whirl of locks and knobs and a strange unreal man who knew him, yet didn't have a name, who seemed to be endlessly referred to as "our man" and nothing more. They were all churning together in panic with a suitcase and the white dazzle of floodlights along a dark finger of boarded jetty.

He said at last, "He knows me. This man ..."

"Yes. Name of Welch. Only a youngster you and me might say. Twenty-two he is. A drifter. You know the type, I expect, well enough. No family, no job, no conscience, no guts, no settled home, no nothing. The sort ... the sort that could vanish without a trace, if you follow me."

George nearly asked, "Are you deliberately needling me? Reminding me that the description could apply to Irene Suttle, too?" The words were there, ready for utterance, and he knew he would have made the colossal, the utterly ridiculous, error of speaking them, only Englebert spoke again.

"I took him over it till he and me must have sounded like a pair of trained cockies." Again that rumble of mirth disturbed the air, but not the blank suntanned features. "He continued being dead sure. He could even tell me the number of your waggon. Funny thing was, it seemed to ring a bell somewhere, but I couldn't remember. However, one of the constables reminded me."

He stopped dead, cocked his head slightly as though trying for a new and perhaps intelligent view of the painting, and went on, "Few weeks back there was a complaint from Moorina. About twelve miles from here, that is, southwards and a mite inland."

"I know," the words were out before he had thought it might be better to go on being silent.

Englebert nodded, cocked his head to the other side to give the painting another long stare. "Complainant talked to her local man who passed it our way, as they found out who owned the car, but as there didn't seem any need ... well, a'ter all, if we attended to every deserted animal we'd never get time for important things. Like parking offences," the rumble left his face untouched as before, "and thieving and missing persons. Only reason it was followed as far as it was was because she went to the trouble of getting the car number and gave a good description of the car and yourself, Mr. Winton." His gaze went suddenly to George's face and stayed there.

"The local man followed it up to the extent of tracing the number and giving it to us. But there, you hadn't wanted the cat or you wouldn't have left it, would you?

So where was the point of making you take it back? Any-way, ladies tend to get attached to cats, wouldn't you say, which is why I expect you left it at that café. But would you mind telling me, Mr. Winton, why you left it that way?"

George felt a wild desire to laugh, and was instantly, with that fatal flicking backwards of memory, remember-ing Kiley's confession of the truth and the way he himself had laughed himself to tears. He tried to fight down the ridiculous wave of mirth; tried to think clearly; tried to go over every word the other man had said, to straighten out his thoughts before he answered.

Finally he said lamely, "I didn't want it, you see. So I left it there. There was an old lady. She looked kind."

He realized that he had been a fool. He had drunk coffee in the café and stayed quite a while. There had been plenty of time for the two women and the man in the filling station to note the car and the number and himself. Perhaps he had seemed on edge, or furtive, to make them note him all the more. Possibly the waitress woman had noticed the way he had peered out at the garden. Perhaps she had thought he was taking too much interest in the place. They might even have thought he was making plans for a later robbery and had watched him, and seen him go out and leave the grey cat.

He said abruptly, "I don't know if I've committed an offence or what. Have I? But I have a dog. It doesn't care for cats. And I couldn't bring myself to destroy the cat, or just leave it somewhere in the scrub, so . . ."

Englebert made a little clicking noise of tongue against teeth. "*That* wouldn't have been nice."

George's head lifted. He knew there was no use trying to fool himself that the other man wasn't, in those slow ponderous sentences, mocking at him. Surprisingly the knowledge helped to settle him. The thudding panic against his ribs subsided and he could think clearly again, reminding himself that there was nothing Englebert could do to him. True, he had now admitted to deserting a cat. But there was nothing in that. He hadn't annoyed the old lady. If she hadn't wanted the cat she could have got rid of it. As to the episode of the books and the case—it was his word against that of a convicted thief.

He said briskly, "If the ... woman ... doesn't want the animal I'll go over and take it back and find some other home for it somewhere."

"Oh she's grown quite fond of it, Mr. Winton. I went over myself just to see."

George looked up sharply. The policeman's tone had been quite pleasant and casual, but the words were ridiculous. The thought of a policeman going twelve miles to ask about the welfare of a cat was laughable, but now he didn't feel in the least like laughing.

Englebert took two steps forward, towards the painting and the wall. He cocked his head again as though hoping for one last look that might bring intelligent enlightenment as to what it was, as he said, "Miss Suttle had a cat like that. It disappeared when she did. And a funny thing— her neighbours say *your* cat and *her* cat're all the same cat."

. . .

Annie stirred, blinking up sleepily. She murmured, "Mmm?"

He said, "Just fruit picking season. He came about that. Just like yesterday," and wondered how long he could keep it from her, whether he should tell her now, or hope that the whole thing would fizzle out with no harm done to anyone.

He sat there beside her, apparently immersed in the papers, remembering Englebert's change of mood and his pressing. "Mr. Winton, are you sure you've never met this Irene Suttle?" asked over and over again in a dozen different versions of the one question.

But he had kept to his first denial. He didn't know her, he had never met her, he had no idea where she was at that moment, and he had never disposed of anything for her, cat or personal possessions, at her request. He had kept to that, and to his impatient comment that one grey cat was very much like any other grey cat, and that one green station waggon was very much like another so that a man who thieved from any car handy could well mix up what he had taken from one with something he had taken from another.

And in the end he had burst out, "But what does it matter, for heaven's sake? Have her family reported her missing? Or her fiancé, perhaps? Or someone like that? The police have this evidence of hers. She must have signed some sort of statement at the time. Surely your confounded inquest can go ahead without . . ."

Englebert had retorted, "A man's dead, and it's a matter now of a possible arrest. When a person's excited, right after an accident, and not on oath, they tend to say a whole heap they wouldn't repeat later in court, *on* oath, especially when there's someone dead. And her going off this way . . . it might be, mightn't it, that what she said wasn't the truth and when she found someone was dead she was scared of admitting she'd lied."

George had asked, "Have you got some notion that she came to me and asked me to hide her out because she's scared to death of admitting she told a few lies. That's ridiculous!"

Englebert had answered only, "I want to know where she is. That's all, Mr. Winton. The whole lot. Let me know where she is and that's the end of it."

There had been only one thing to answer. He had said it.

"I don't know where she is," he had claimed, and had known that he wasn't believed.

CHAPTER TWELVE

THEY had, in the last few weeks, taken to breakfasting in bed, because Annie's pregnancy had inclined her towards what she called morning laziness, and because for him the morning, without Annie there beside him to comment laughingly on the contents of the newspapers, wasn't complete. Even on that Monday morning, with memories of a haunted night behind him, he could smile at her comment on details of a politician's banquet. "Must be pregnant, the whole mob of them," she told him, biting into toast, "and old-fashioned with it—believing in eating enough for two, though I'd say by the sound of this the whole mob's expecting quins and eating for six."

"They don't have to pay for it," he reminded absently.

"Sooner or later you always pay for whatever you get up to," she told him smugly. "This lot now—I bet they burped all the way home."

He hoped desperately that she wouldn't look up and see his face. He was sure that the smile was fixed there and that there was sweat on his forehead.

"Sooner or later . . . you always pay . . . for whatever you get up to." The words seemed to repeat themselves endlessly over and over again, while Annie went on chattering without him hearing a word of it.

He knew there was no point in trying to hide from her the paragraph that had claimed his attention. After a little he touched her arm. The flesh was warm and soft under his fingers, and abruptly his hand dragged away as the retching thought came to him of flesh cold from the sea and death. He said thickly, "Annie . . ."

He pointed silently to the paragraph. He heard her indrawn breath, then she was quiet. After a moment she said almost wonderingly, "The police want her," but there was no fear mixed up with the wonder, only surprise and puzzlement and he was suddenly angry that she hadn't understood that the little paragraph stating the police were anxious to interview Irene Suttle, meant that now a search, relentless, determined, unstoppable, was going on for the dead woman; that across miles of bush and desert and coastline, through cities and shanty towns and quiet country areas, wherever there were police, the news would have reached out and been filed away and acted on.

"It says," Annie went on, "they want her because they think she can give them valuable information—and what does that mean ever?—about some accident. Well," she pushed the paper a little aside, "they won't find her, that's all."

He wondered if she was deliberately closing her mind to factors she didn't want to face. He said flatly, "and they're going to wonder why, Annie. When they can't find her and she doesn't answer that appeal, or get in touch with friends or anyone else . . . they're going to wonder why."

He knew, quite definitely now, that the police would return and keep returning. They'd question him and they'd question Annie, and she had to be prepared for it. He started speaking and felt her soft body gradually tensing against his side. Even his arm, holding her close against his own body, couldn't help her.

Then she said defiantly, "They can't do anything, George love, they can't. What's a cat? And a bit of a suitcase? And a book with a name in it? They can't do anything," and then her defiance broke with a low-voiced, "can they?"

"The only thing they can do is make life uncomfortable," he told her bluntly. "Englebert seems convinced I've hidden her because she lied about this confounded accident. Because he thinks that, he thinks there's something completely fishy about that evidence she gave on it before. Don't you see, Annie, the police wouldn't dare arrest someone for causing a man's death in a car accident if they thought her evidence was a lie and any minute it might be *proved* to be a lie. The police aren't going to simply shrug this off—they're going to do their damnedest to find her. They'll harass me. They'll harass you. There are a lot of ways they can do that—not just questioning us, but our friends . . . asking if we knew Irene Suttle; where we might have hidden her?"

"And then what?" she asked. "When it all comes down to nothing, what then?"

"They'll have to give up. Eventually."

He hoped that she wasn't, as he had done, wondering what it would be like to live for uncounted time ahead under police suspicion, under the veiled curiosity of neighbours and friends who had been questioned about them, and under a barrage of whispers that would tear without compunction at their privacy.

She asked abruptly, "Are you going to get in touch with Evan and Miriam Kiley?"

"I tried, on Saturday," he told her, "but they've moved, heaven knows where, and when you come to look at it, Annie, what's the point of reaching them? Short of telling the truth they can't do a thing."

"He could say he saw her leave. Alone. That she told him she was going away and that . . ."

"If she left alone she could still have met up with me and I could still be hiding her. It's not a case of them thinking her dead. She's disappeared, and they think she lied and that I'm hiding her," he reminded.

Her hand traced along the curve of his jaw and suddenly her warm voice was exultant.

"They'll soon see that's a lot of baloney, George love.

Oh yes, they will! See, if they've that idea in their heads they must think you and she were carrying on behind my back or all three of us were close as wedges of pie. Or we wouldn't have a reason for hiding her out, now would we? And they'll find it was never so and they'll know they were wrong."

She was right of course, he realized, but strangely the thought gave little comfort. He could only wonder what the police would think when they discovered that fact and were still left with the grey cat and a thief's story.

• • •

He had never become used to the miracle of the wide-windowed office, and the knowledge that the whole place revolved round himself; never become used to the fact that that first attempt at independence, a run-down building bought with borrowed money and turned slowly into a motel with his own sweating hands, had mushroomed and grown to the present chain of comfortable, middle-priced motels that bore his name. He had once said to Annie that he thought his success had been half luck and half because he had never ventured into the world of luxury and high prices. He had known, and confessed it bluntly to Annie, that to a world of luxury he and his ideas would be totally wrong. He had built for people of his own stamp and rearing, feeling that he knew into their minds and knew what to them was a luxury of living quite remote from real luxury, and success had come, sweeping him and Annie to comfort and more than comfort.

Sweeping them, too, he suddenly remembered that morning, into the terror of Victoria's going, the worse terror and despair of Kiley's coming and now . . . his mind closed down on the thought of what the future might hold as he stood up and faced Englebert and a stranger.

He had expected to see Englebert again some time that

Monday. He had been sure the man would come to question and needle him all over again, but he hadn't expected the stranger, or that the pair of them would turn up as soon as the Winton offices were open.

He nodded to Englebert and waited, silently, still standing, till the policeman had introduced his companion. He repeated, gesturing them both to chairs, "Detective-sergeant Gregor. What can I do for you, then?"

"Tell me where Miss Irene Suttle happens to be."

The blunt question came in a brisk, almost harsh voice from the thin plainclothes man.

"Out of the question. I don't know her. I've never met her."

"Some of her possessions were taken from your car."

"According to a convicted thief," George gave back. "I deny it."

Gregor let that point go, retorting, "You left Miss Suttle's cat at a café some twelve miles from here."

"I left *a* cat."

"Identified as hers by former neighbours. It originally belonged to some old lady. Miss Suttle took it and the old woman's cottage over at the same time."

When George remained silent the thin man frowned. The silence lengthened. There was only the sound of a typewriter from somewhere in the outer office, the hum of traffic and the soft whirring of the electric fan in one corner of the office. George knew the silence was meant to unnerve him. He determined it wasn't going to. He concentrated on Gregor, noting the good cut of the summer-weight suit of grey, the narrowness of the dark green tie and the way Gregor's jet black hair was receding, to leave a tide line of paler skin above the deeply suntanned face.

Then the policeman sighed. He said, almost wearily, "Mr. Winton, let me explain something. It isn't criminal for someone to tell a lie. Unless they happen to be on oath, of course, when it turns into perjury. You can give a statement to the police and sign it and later on retract it. We're only too well acquainted with what happens when someone's upset and excited and overcome, maybe, with the novelty of being a witness to something out of the ordinary."

George asked, in sudden curiosity, "Just what was this accident this . . . woman saw?"

"A very simple one, and a very common one, so it seemed at the time. An old gentleman stepped off a footpath and was run down, the driver putting on speed and vanishing without stopping."

"Hit-and-run," George jerked the words out.

"Exactly, Mr. Winton. Hit-and-run. Not at all a pretty crime, but people panic and then . . . anyway, Miss Suttle saw the accident, and was questioned and she described the vehicle—it was a grey Volkswagon panel van and the last two figures of its number were three and four."

"Well?" George broke the sudden silence. He began slowly to polish over the lenses of his glasses, not looking at the plainclothes man.

"Attempts were made, naturally, to find the van. In the meantime the old gentleman was taken to hospital. It was believed then he wasn't seriously hurt, but later on he collapsed and died. Not to go into technicalities, Mr. Winton, there was hidden damage to the brain."

"Well?" the word jerked out into another silence.

"A man was questioned. He drives a grey Volkswagon panel van with the last figures being three and four and he often has to drive through the area where this accident occurred. He had to drive through there that day in question. He admits he did so, but claims his journey happened at least an hour before the time of the accident. He says Miss Suttle must have seen his van that morning, or remembered it from some other time and confused it with the one that caused the accident. As he says, one grey van is very much like another."

"Just," George put in gently, "as one grey cat closely resembles another."

He saw a sudden glint of humour in the brown eyes watching him, but Gregor's face remained quite grave as he said, "I don't deny it. Now . . . the constable who took Miss Suttle's statement at the time said she was very excited, and almost hysterical from shock, which was perhaps natural. She said, though, that she was quite sure she would know the driver if she saw him again and that he had dark hair and spectacles. The driver of this van has dark hair and he wears spectacles for reading and it's quite possible he might have left them on and been wearing them at the time of the accident.

"Again, Miss Suttle was quite definite on one point—she claimed the vehicle swept round the corner at such high speed it was quite unable to stop in time. The old gentleman gave his own statement in hospital. He couldn't describe the vehicle—all he knew was that at one moment the roadway was clear and the next something had turned the corner and was on him. You see, both statements lay the blame completely on the driver.

"So now we need Miss Suttle's evidence. We want her to try and identify the driver and the van."

When George didn't speak he leaned forward. He said urgently, "Mr. Winton, look at it this way. Hit-and-run is a nasty thing. So is dangerous driving. If we don't have Miss Suttle's evidence, we can't take any action. If he's guilty he gets off scot-free. If he's innocent—he carries the slur of suspected hit-and-run for the rest of his life."

George looked down at his hands, clasped together now in front of him on the polished wood top of the desk. He said at length, "But why should she try to hide from you?

She could take back her statement. I don't think the van driver could so much as sue her for damages, could he? So there's hardly any reason ..."

"No, Mr. Winton, there isn't. No reason at all. So just why are you lying? Why won't you tell us where she is?"

•　　•　　•

He debated the attitudes of false anger, of pretended shock, of defiance, of a thousand things, and merely said wearily in the end, "I'm not lying to you. I've never met her. I don't know her."

Gregor threw himself back in his chair as though he was completely exasperated. George went on gazing at him, blank-faced, and finally Gregor said, holding the other man's gaze with his own, "Mr. Winton, will you please reach for that writing pad, and a pen." George had done so before he had time to think of the words and Gregor went on, "Now please write 'No Milk'."

He had started to write the words before the shock reached him. He looked down at the white paper with its black words and instinctively moved to crush it, but Gregor said sharply, "No, Mr. Winton—finish it, please. Now look," his tone was persuasive, "there's no use beating about the bush, Mr. Winton. Your writing is rather distinctive. That capital N for instance. You wrote the note that was tacked to the doorpost of Miss Suttle's house. That means you helped her leave the place."

He didn't have time to think, to work out that it might be better to admit that he had, and then to deny that he knew her present whereabouts. All he could think of was denying everything they flung at him.

He said, "No. That's not so."

"Mr. Winton," Gregor was leaning forward again, "turn your mind back to the early morning of the seventeenth of last month, will you? When something was taken

133

from your station waggon at the marina. Where did you take your boat that dawn?"

"Just out to sea."

"You went fishing?"

In time he remembered what he had already told Engle-bert. He shook his head. "No, I was taking some rubbish out to dump it."

"You were alone?"

"No." He hesitated after the swift denial. He saw the quick glance passing between them and said in sudden anger, "For pity's sake, get it out of your heads that I wafted the woman off to some hiding-hole. The whole thing's so ridiculous it's laughable."

"Who was with you?"

He hesitated again. He didn't want to mention Kiley, but he couldn't right then think of anyone he could name and know for a certainty they would back him up and wouldn't prove to have been elsewhere at the time. Finally he said, "A man by the name of Evan Kiley."

"Kiley?" Gregor was frowning, "Of Comboroo?"

"Yes."

He realized then, in sickening dismay, what he had done. He knew what Gregor would say next, even before the words were framed and spoken.

"You mean you know this Kiley, but not his next door neighbour, Miss Suttle?"

He felt relief in the quickness of thought that made him ask boldly, "*Was* she his next door neighbour? I didn't know. I've told you I didn't know her. Good lord, do you know the neighbours of everyone you visit, man?"

"You're on visiting terms with Kiley then?"

He hesitated, then nodded.

"You're close friends?"

"No, though I can't see," he gave back angrily, "that it concerns you." More slowly he added, "It happens I

134

was doing business with Kiley. There's to be a new building—road and bridge building—that way and I was interested in getting in early and buying up land there for a possible motel in the future. Kiley had land for sale. I bought it."

"So your relationship is strictly business?"

"Yes."

"I thought," Gregor demanded, "that you said your trip was to let you get rid of some rubbish?"

"That's right." He was surprised at how easily and fluently he was able to lie now. "Kiley had expressed interest in my boat, as he was thinking of using the money I'd paid for his land on a boat of his own. He wanted to have the handling of mine, but the weather had been bad. That night it was good. I thought Kiley might as well come." He blew smoke gently across the space between them. "Our business was completed, and, frankly, I didn't see Kiley and myself extending our friendship. I thought I might as well get the job of showing him the boat over and done with."

He felt something akin to disinterest as the two men rose. He knew it wasn't over; that they'd come back. He saw them out and tried to turn to work. It was only when he saw the surprise on the plump face of his secretary that he realized his face was cold with sweat and that his hands, handling the papers in front of him, were trembling so that the sheets rustled.

He told her to go and knew that soon it would be a choice item of gossip that the Mogul—he knew quite well they all called him that behind his back—had had the police in his office and was quivering like aspic.

Abruptly he pressed the switch recalling her. He told her to get him the file on the Comboroo land and when it came he told her to get him the Comboroo lawyer who had handled Kiley's interest.

His conversation was brief. When he put down the phone he knew that Kiley had gone interstate to Sydney, but he didn't know whether to use the knowledge or not. He couldn't see that discussion would help at all. Kiley, if the police contacted him, could confirm the trip; could confirm that Irene Suttle hadn't been aboard, and then he could step aside. He could deny all knowledge of what had been taken on board, and the police could do nothing to him.

And it had been imperative to bring Kiley into it. He could see that quite clearly. If he had denied ever being in Comboroo there would have been the land sale record to call him a liar. It had been better to admit quite frankly that he had been to the house next door to Irene Suttle's.

He tried to still fear as he sat there, with a memory of Annie's defiant, "They can't do anything to you, George love," but fear wouldn't go. He kept remembering shrewd brown eyes and a voice saying, "No, Mr. Winton, there isn't any reason. Not really. So just why are you lying? Why won't you tell us where she is?"

CHAPTER THIRTEEN

WHEN he and Annie finally went to bed that night, when they had talked it all over and she had fallen asleep with her red head pillowed in the hollow of his shoulder, he knew only bewilderment and anger and fear. He was no longer trying to look ahead, or even behind him. The only thing he knew for certain was that in the morning he would fly to Sydney and he would see Kiley and demand a reason for the other man's lying.

He had expected all that day that the police would come back to the office. He had even put aside two long-made appointments because he had expected that and he had wanted to get whatever was coming over and done with, but they hadn't come, and when he had gone home expecting Annie to say they had been there, that hadn't happened either.

He might have known, he thought afterwards, that they would lull him into a faint feeling of security; wait till tiredness had taken over his body and mind, and then come back with their questions. They had come at half past nine, and he had been half asleep, in the black leather chair, with Annie curled up on the floor beside him, her arms white against the black of the leather.

They had asked to see him alone and he had wondered, as he had led the way silently into the long sun-room at the back of the house, if they had guessed it would have been easier for him with Annie's presence there at his side; with her warm voice in her ear, with her championing if she had thought him threatened.

He had opened the conversation himself with a blunt, "It's late. I have to be up early tomorrow."

"So do I, Mr. Winton." That had been Gregor. "So we'll keep things as brief as possible. Will you tell me how you came to be mistaken about your trip out to sea in the early morning of the seventeenth?"

He had stared blankly at them, then parroted, "Mistaken?" demanding, "What about?"

"About the company you had. Mr. Kiley denies he was with you that morning."

He had felt only bewilderment. He was sure it had shown on his face when he had retorted, "Then it's Kiley who's mistaken. He went out with me on the *Heron* . . ."

"On the eighteenth, Mr. Winton. He's quite sure about it. We asked the Sydney police to interview him. He's quite clear about it. He told us frankly he knows the date because on the night of the sixteenth his wife came home after an absence of some months. There'd been a quarrel and they made it up that night—that night that covers the early morning of the seventeenth, Mr. Winton. He says he's certain it was the next night that you and he went out."

There had still been only bewilderment in him. He had tried to work out if Kiley had been told what was happening in the north and had decided it was better to claim it had been the following night—better to deny that he and George had ever been on the marina on the morning of the seventeenth. Anger had come then, at Kiley for so confusing things; followed by despair because of course Kiley could not have known what to do for the best. He had stood there telling himself he had been a fool not to get in touch with Kiley immediately, then Gregor had gone on:

"Perhaps you didn't go out on the early morning of the eighteenth at all? Is that what *you* claim?"

"No." His denial had been swift. "I went out then, too." But he hadn't elaborated, and Gregor hadn't pressed the point, so there had been no need to think of a lie to cover that morning of despair, when he had lain awake all night and stolen out before dawn to go across the dark sea again, with that nightmare in his mind that perhaps the body would have risen in spite of the weights he and Kiley had tied to it, and that it would be rolling there in the rise and fall of the sapphire sea, an indecent, obscene exposure of what he and Kiley had done.

"Then you've mixed your dates," Gregor had told him, and without giving him time to argue had added, "Jacobs at the marina said you were alone on the morning of the seventeenth. There was no one with you. He saw you carrying aboard a case and a small trunk, and it's an odd thing, Mr. Winton—you described that as something between a large case and a small trunk to Englebert here. The solicitors who let the cottage in Comboroo to Miss Suttle say their man went with her to open the house when she first arrived. He helped her in with her luggage. There were two cases and something between a large case and a small trunk."

He had managed, "There must be thousands of boxes like that. They must be all of a kind—all of a . . . ."

"Like grey cats, Mr. Winton," Gregor had broken in smoothly, "Mr. Kiley now says when he was with you he helped you toss over old wooden palings and a few oddments—nothing more."

George had silently cursed Kiley for the man's efforts to help and smooth things out. He had wished desperately then that he and Kiley could have talked so he would have known what had been in the younger man's mind when he had said that.

He had remained silent when Gregor continued, "And Jacobs says you had something else—a long bundle. Something very heavy, so he says. He said you were alone. He could hear your steps. Just the one set. Staggering, so he says, as though you were struggling along with something heavy. At first he thought it was the thief getting away with something. He waited till the steps stopped, expecting, when the lights went on, to see the man searching for his rowboat. Instead he saw you, on the *Heron's* deck."

It had all come back to him so vividly — Kiley in sand-shoes and himself in leather-soled shoes and that appalling noise. His steps had drowned out Kiley's of course and when the lights had gone on — he remembered how Kiley had been behind him and had ducked down, shielding his eyes. No wonder Jacobs had thought him alone, he had reflected and then Gregor had demanded, "Mr. Winton, what was that long, heavy, covered object you took on board?"

He had known the sudden tide of colour coming and draining away from his features must have been visible to the two men. In the end he had said lamely, "Old scraps of carpeting. They've been around for . . . oh, a long time."

The next question had been such a surprise he had simply gaped for a moment. He had expected Gregor to keep harping on the *Heron's* trip. Instead he had asked, "Mr. Winton, on your way to seeing Mr. Kiley, you'd drive through Comboroo from the northern road, wouldn't you?"

After a little, puzzled, he had simply nodded.

"Would you have driven down there on the second of last month?"

That had been easy. He had said, "No!" sharply, almost eagerly, because it was one question he could answer truthfully.

"How can you be sure?" Gregor had pressed.

"Because I didn't go to Comboroo till some time after that. I hadn't heard of the place."

Gregor had cocked an eyebrow in patent disbelief.

"Yet a short while later you bought land there. You must have looked the area over — been convinced it was suitable, mustn't you, Mr. Winton? There was a story about Comboroo and the possibility of a new bridge and highway to it, in the papers at the end of the previous month. Wasn't there, Mr. Winton? As a good business man you would have noted that and driven out as quickly as possible, wouldn't you, to get ahead of any rival concern, and . . . well, I suppose spy out the road, is the term, isn't it?"

He had added complacently, when George remained silent, "So it's quite likely you would be there, that way, on the second, wouldn't it now? And you were out of your office that day, weren't you? Your secretary says so," he had finished with bland indifferent to the growing anger that George had known was showing in his own expression.

He had started furiously, "You had no right to . . ." then had cooled down and tried to shrug the matter aside with a quiet, "I was Ireland's Bay way, probably. I've been interested in a mild way in possibilities there." Anger had given way to a gnawing anxiety as to what the questions meant. Finally he had asked.

Gregor had told him, "That's the day when Irene Suttle saw a man run down by a hit-and-run driver."

Surprise had swept over him again, in a startled, "But good lord, what's that to do with me?"

Even now, lying beside Annie, when he had told her everything and they had clung together in an agony of apprehension, he could hardly believe that Gregor had actually put tongue to the enormity.

"Mr. Winton, we can't find Miss Suttle and it's quite obvious you must have some idea, at least, as to where she happens to be. Her possessions were in your station waggon, you disposed of her cat, your handwriting is the same as on the note on her door." He shook his head. "No, Mr. Winton, please don't argue that tired point about coincidence. One coincidence is possible—three I cannot swallow.

"So she's disappeared and as you pointed out this morning, why on earth should she? If she told the truth, so far as she knew it, about that accident, and has panicked at the idea of appearing in court, *you* wouldn't be lying in this fashion. The idea is patently ridiculous.

"That leaves the question of her having lied. She could have done so because she honestly mixed up the make and type of vehicle with one she had seen somewhere else. Secondly, she might have lied deliberately out of a need to be important and to seek the limelight, but in neither case would she need to disappear or have you lying about her whereabouts.

"You must see, Mr. Winton, how it appears to us." He had leaned forward, his brown eyes holding George's fascinated gaze. "If you are hiding her and she remains hidden, doesn't it seem that she must know something about *you* that you cannot afford to have come out? Couldn't it be that she knew quite well who caused that accident? A man known to her as someone wealthy? And that she lied, said the first thing that came into her head to the investigating police, rather than admit the truth."

He had known he couldn't go on sitting there while the brisk voice needled and probed at him. He had said bluntly, "You mean, you think I ran down that old man and she knew it and decided to find out how much I'd pay for her to keep quiet about it, don't you?"

When Gregor had remained silent, George had exploded into rage. He had known afterwards that they had wanted him to do that—to lose his head and perhaps say too much. If they had expected that, though, they had been disappointed, because even in that wild gust of rage all he had said was "The whole thing's impossible! If you had the brains of a nit you'd know it, man. If this wretched woman was blackmailing me, why would I hide her out? Wouldn't I rather pay her all she wanted to stand up in court and say simply she made a mistake about that van, while remaining quiet about myself? Because she'd admitted lying about the van doesn't mean she would have to say *I* did it. Are you so dumb you can't see that, or are you just trying to needle me?"

He had crushed out his cigarette in disgust, prodding and crushing at it with his fingers till it was a torn and draggled mass in the ashtray. The two men had watched him in silence and had remained silent till George had finally burst out, "Why the devil should I be hiding her?"

Then Gregor had nodded. He had said quietly, "That's the point, Mr. Winton, why should you?" and then he had demanded, "What was in that long heavy bundle you had such difficulty in loading on to the *Heron*, Mr. Winton?"

CHAPTER FOURTEEN

THE city had lain under a pall of fog that morning and
the plane had circled over the thick grey-white blanket of
it for over half an hour, but that had still left him time
enough to make his appointment with Kiley; time and
enough so that he was there first.

Kiley had chosen Hyde Park, explaining it was close to
his office; that he and Miriam hadn't settled in anywhere
and were simply boarding in what he called "depressed
suburbia" till they found a house. There hadn't been time
to talk in the limited minutes of the previous day's phone
call. Even if there had been, George was sure that Kiley
would have grudged the time and the words.

After the first surprise expressed in a jerked, "Winton?
Of all people . . ." he had said very little, but in that little
he had made it clear he thought the meeting was point-
less. But George, when he had made the call, had felt a
need to talk things over, to clarify what both were going to
say. He hadn't known, when he made it, the full enormity
of what the police were thinking. If he had, he would have
gone on talking while the minutes raced by uncounted.

At that early hour, under the greyness of fog, with
moisture over gaily-painted seats, dripping from the trees,
clinging to the statues of the fountain, the park had shed
its normal summer-time crowds. There were a few people,
faces bent frowningly towards unknown destinations, who
passed him without a glance, and a white-stubbled
creased face that peered at him dully as its owner picked
over the leavings in a waste-bin. In swift revulsion at the
sight he turned away, hurrying, though there was plenty
of time, towards the Pool of Reflection. The surface of the

water had taken on the tinge of the fog—grey and flat and oily, like a dulled mirror. He stood staring down into it and didn't hear Kiley come.

Only when the voice asked, "Well?" did he look up and turn.

Kiley looked different. That was his first thought, then he realized why that impression had come. Always before, Kiley's freckled long face had expressed some emotion— tiredness, grief, anger, a thousand things. Now its angles seemed to have filled out. His face looked rounder and smooth and blank of expression.

"Well?" he said again, without any greeting.

"Kiley, we've got to talk," he said lamely.

The other man nodded. He was wearing a neat grey suit that might have been a replica of George's own. George found his thoughts wandering, reflecting that the two of them could have been business men discussing some point with only the pigeons to hear.

"Well?" Kiley asked again.

George looked away. He found it difficult to start talking now with that shuttered face opposite his eyes. In the single word, in the blank smooth face, even in the place of meeting, he knew that Kiley was showing him he had closed his life to the Wintons and all their concerns. He wanted them to close their life to himself in return. He was resenting the new intrusion and wanted it over as quickly as possible.

George found himself speaking almost apologetically.

"It isn't my fault I had to see you again. But we have to talk, Kiley. This business . . . you know they're looking for *her*, of course."

Kiley merely nodded. He was staring upwards, gaze moving slowly towards the top of the Anzac Memorial and returning to the pool.

George pressed on desperately, anger taking over,

"Why the dickens did you lie about that trip out on the *Heron*? They told me they'd asked you about it and you said it was the eighteenth, not the seventeenth, when we went out. Did you have some idea that was going to make things better—prove we weren't at the marina on the seventeenth? You've left me . . ."

"They showed me her case. They wanted to know if I recognized it; whether I saw it in your car the night we went to the marina; whether you took anything on board."

He stopped and George's thoughts wandered again—this time to the fact that both he and Kiley seemed averse to mentioning the dead woman by name.

"I said," Kiley went on, "I'd never seen it before, and that I didn't know what you had in your car."

"And I'd told them I was taking some rubbish out to sea, to dump it. Jacobs—the caretaker on the marina—saw me lugging the trunk and the case."

"Listen, how did they get onto the fact that case was hers? And how'd they get hold of it? They didn't tell me and I didn't ask. I played pussyfooting through the tulips and pretended I was just surprised, and all they gave me was you'd reported some stuff stolen and they thought this might be it—a real run-around, but I knew they were looking for her. They were after me weeks ago wanting to know where she was and did I have an idea? And I saw that press call for her, too."

"The thief came back to the marina and was caught. The case and her brush and comb and a couple of books with her name in it were in his room. He said they came out of my car that dawn at the marina."

Kiley swore softly. "Wouldn't it give you the gripe to think the books had to be in that case. What did you say?"

"That I'd never seen the case or the other things. What else could I give them? They seemed to think I had her on board—I expected you to say you were with me and that we were alone. What was the point of saying it was the following night we went out?"

Kiley shrugged. He was looking down into the grey water. George could see the wavering reflection of both their faces. As he continued gazing a faint sparkle of light touched the water and he looked up, seeing the fog was beginning to lift and the sun was filtering through. The two of them continued to stand there, silent, while the light grew brighter and the world stirred. Pigeons shook themselves and preened, strutting hopefully in search of crumbs; the stone of the memorial changed from dulled grey to pearl; a girl went by in a flick of pink swirling skirts, untangling her arms from a blue plastic mac as she went, her face uplifted towards the faint light, and an old man shuffled to a nearby seat, carefully spread newspaper on its damp surface and sat, knees apart, hands folded on stick, eyes closed, but face expectant of coming warmth.

George asked again, "What was the point of saying our trip was the next night? You'll have to recant, and say it was the previous dawn, say you saw what I took on board, that it was old rubbish in a case and trunk and that you helped me dump it and that . . ."

"No."

When he turned Kiley's face was quite smooth still.

He said again, "No." Then after a little he added, "Listen, George, stop hiding your head in the sand. I'm in the clear in this and I'm staying in the clear. Get it? Her case was found in your car. Alright? So what? I wasn't there. I know nothing about it. Or her. Or anything else. Except I took a trip with you one dawn and all we pitched over was a bit of rubbish—wood and stuff. If you pitched a trunk and case over, you did it without me seeing. I'm certain that caretaker bloke didn't catch sight of me. To him you were alone . . ."

147

"He's already told the police so. That I was alone. That I was . . ."

"You see, then? I'm in the clear. And I'm not stepping forward to tell them a different tale than I've told already and have them ask about the stuff that you took aboard. You say the caretaker chap saw the things, and this chap who pinched the case saw them, too. You can tell what story you like to explain it all, providing you leave me right out of it."

He wasn't surprised. He had thought it might be that way—that Kiley had seen a way of keeping himself and Miriam well away from police questioning. He wasn't even angry about it as he said, "But you don't know the whole of it, Kiley. You see . . . they think . . . wait on though, do you know why they're looking for her?"

"That accident." Kiley nodded. He was looking upwards now, too, at the space where fog had rolled back and blue sky was showing. He took a deep breath, as though the warmth was seeping deep into his body. "She told me about that. Went in one ear and out the other at the time. She made a great hoo-haa, but it wasn't worth a cent. We hardly gave it space in the paper at the time. The old chap didn't seem hurt."

"Did she really see the grey van and the driver or was that a figment of . . ."

Kiley shrugged. "Possibly. She was a bit addled, actually. About anything. If she got excited, I mean. She might have seen it or a red fire engine. I wouldn't know. It just didn't seem important. Then. So I didn't listen."

"It's important now," George told him swiftly. He went on speaking, urgently, willing Kiley to look down; to let some expression into the smooth freckled face upturned towards the widening patch of blue. But Kiley didn't look down. He didn't look anywhere but at the sky, and his face remained quite blank of expression.

When George had told him the lot, finishing in a desperate urgency that made him almost stutter the words, "They've got the idea I was the hit-and-run driver; that she knew; that I've got rid of her; that I took her out to sea that night and disposed of her," Kiley still looked up at the sky.

He said evenly, "Why, that's too bad, George."

"Too bad," he uttered the words as though he found them unreal. He asked in amazement, "Aren't you frightened?"

"No, George," Kiley said softly. "Why should I be? Listen, George," he looked down suddenly and his pale eyes were quite cold, "I'm in the clear. I've told you that. And I'm staying in the clear. I'm not going to say I was with you because on your admission the caretaker thinks you took a body aboard, and that thief can prove you had her things—or one case full of them anyway; and that woman can prove you left that cat out there—what the blazes possessed you to do a fool thing like that, anyway?"

When the elder man didn't answer Kiley went on evenly, "but none of it touches me, George. *I* didn't leave the damn cat; *I* didn't pen that note—and what possessed you there, again? And *I* didn't have her cases and *I* wasn't seen on board the *Heron* that night. Get it? I'm clear, George, and I'm staying clear. No matter what. I know you feel sick as you look, but there it is. All I'm concerned with is Miriam. It's no good me recanting my yarn now and saying I was with you that night. They probably believe you took rubbish on the eighteenth, probably to confuse me on the dates. I can't help it. If I recant they either don't believe me or they believe me and think I had a hand in getting rid of her, too.

"The only way we can get out of it is by telling the truth. I'm not doing it."

Then his voice softened. It was almost soothing as he

149

said, "Listen, George, you've nothing really to worry over. They'll pester you right enough and it'll be uncomfortable, but *they can't prove anything*. You get a grip on that. There's not a thing they can prove. They haven't got a body and they can't get one, because she's at the bottom of the sea."

"You mean you're not going to do a thing to help, or try to help? You're going to make me and Annie face the questioning and the talk and . . . I think they could arrest me. Even without a body I think they could . . . there must be cases where there hasn't been a body." His voice was rising, but he couldn't stop it. There was only frantic fear in him, for himself and for Annie and for Victoria. They'd all be involved if he was arrested; all have to face the talk and the sneers and the slurs, and even if he was let go in the end, even if he wasn't even arrested at all, there'd always be talk. He was suddenly reminded of Gregor saying urgently, when speaking of the driver of the grey van, "if he's innocent he'll have to live with the slur of hit-and-run for the rest of his life."

"They couldn't make anything stick," Kiley said in that same soothing voice.

"You can't know it. And mud sticks," he pressed desperately.

"People have short memories and you've good compensation." Kiley's mouth had a sudden unpleasant twist. "Let's face it, George, if my land comes good you've made a clear forty thousand profit. Oh yes, I know I named my price and that was that, but I notice that afterwards you never made a move to let me have the land back, or alter the price. You must have had a solicitors' letter to say the sale was complete. I had one. I thought you might write and offer me the land back or a better price. When you didn't . . ." he shrugged, "I put it down as compensation to you and Annie. You'd had quite a time and it was my fault, or Miriam's. So I let it ride, but let's face it, George, you could have altered things if you'd wanted to. You didn't want. You were quite happy at the idea of a nice little profit. So don't squeal now. Think of that coming profit and take the questioning. It won't last for ever, and they can't prove a thing. Just as I said."

He turned on his heel; started to move away. He flung back at George's red, angry face, "Don't get in touch with me again. It won't be any use."

"What are you going to do if I'm arrested?" George took two steps after him.

"What would you expect me to do? Weep?"

"Tell the truth. If I'm arrested, Annie will suffer too and Victoria—kids can be murder to other kids when something . . ."

"Send them away for a while. It's no good, George, I'm out of this and I'm staying out. I'll tell you this much— Miriam's had a sort of breakdown. She's my sole concern. Not you. And remember you've got good compensation for it all."

"I left it to you to get in touch with me if you wanted things altered," George said. He knew the words, and his voice were feeble. He was cursing himself for that reluctance to have anything more to do with the Kileys; for letting things slide until he knew if the land would fetch a higher price. "I would have given you the full price as soon as things were definite. It's still in the air, even now."

"So you say, George. It doesn't matter. I just don't want to hear from you again. Get it?"

"Kiley," George went after him again. He saw the impatience, the frown, on the freckled face that looked back. He said flatly, "I could tell the truth myself, remember."

He saw the sudden smile that touched Kiley's mouth,

then the younger man shrugged. "Who'd believe you? You haven't one single shred of proof, George."

Then he was gone, hurrying away across the grass. George went on standing there, then walked slowly back to the pool. His whole body seemed burning, but when he looked into the water the wavering reflection was as pale as ever.

He began to move slowly away, passing the seat where the old man was sitting, eyes wide open now as he surveyed a scolding of sparrows in a nearby patch of grey-brown dust. He smiled gently as the younger man went by and George forced his own features into an answering smile.

He wondered as he walked out of the park into the now blazing sunshine pouring onto the city streets if the old man would pick up his paper one day soon and see a photograph and remember that morning and the fixed, painful smile that had turned to him.

CHAPTER FIFTEEN

THE two of them had talked it over and over and over till every word that Kiley had said to him and all he had said to Kiley seemed to him to hang there in the still hot air of the bedroom. The night had brought a heatwave which the whirring fan did little to help. He and Annie had tossed back even the light top sheet, but in spite of the sticky clamminess of his body she clung to him. He could feel the harsh breath fluttering against his neck, and the pounding of her heart under the soft flesh and strangely, in that moment, he felt no anger against Kiley. He thought of the other man, in what he had called "depressed suburbia" in some furnished room, holding Miriam close in the same way and feeling her heart beats of fear.

Annie asked, the words hardly audible, "What are we going to do? George love ..."

"Oh god, I don't know." His clasp on her tightened. "Even if I managed to prove what I'm telling is the truth, there's still that girl ... they'd arrest her then. They'd send her to prison for a certainty. There's only her word for it that *she* ..." he stopped, realizing he had again side-tracked the use of the dead woman's name, "that Irene Suttle," he said slowly, "that Irene Suttle asked to be tied up. They might say Miriam had someone with her ..."

"That cousin," she breathed against his ear. "The one who cared for the little boy."

He didn't answer and after a little she said, almost in bewilderment, "But there must be something he can do. If the two of you only put your wits to work ... he'd have to be willing to back you up if you told some tale together, and see," her fingers dug urgently into his arm, "it'll suit him just as fine as us if this is over quick-smart, so he's sure..."

"I don't see how it's possible to tell any tale to explain away that confounded cat, or the suitcases or that note on her door and when you come to look at it closely, Annie, Kiley's right in saying if he admitted to being on the *Heron* it wouldn't help. The police would think he was in it with me, or they might think he was quite innocent—that I used him to prove I threw rubbish overboard when I had more than that waiting to be tossed over."

He added after a little, "Either I ride it out and take the consequences and hope it all blows over, or I tell the truth and let the police make what they can of it. I don't think they'd believe me. If they did ... Miriam Kiley's going to suffer. It boils down to that. I've no choice, Annie," he said helplessly, "I've just *got* to ride it out and see what comes."

"You could maybe find that cousin. Miriam Kiley's cousin," her soft voice urged, but there was doubt and despair to equal his own in the suggestion, "maybe he'd admit that ..."

"He wouldn't, Annie. Why should he? He wouldn't hurt his cousin and if he told what he knew he could be arrested himself—you said a minute ago, remember, that the police might think Miriam had someone with her and used violence because *she* wouldn't let the boy go with his mother."

"Then," her hand traced along the line of his jaw in gentle caress, and her mouth smiled below her fear-stricken eyes, "we just ride it, huh? And hope we haven't stepped on an outlaw who'll toss us down to the dirt."

• • •

It began next morning—the slanted looks, the long curious stares that turned away immediately he felt them and looked round to see who was taking a close interest in his movements. The office, from a place of quiet efficiency, was suddenly a place of whispers and hastily averted eyes.

Even Helen Stone, the plump-faced, middle-aged woman who had once worked with him behind the desk of a second-grade hotel and was now his secretary, seemed affected by it. When his suddenly raised gaze sent her own skittering hastily towards the wall over his head, he pushed the papers that they had been discussing and said tightly, "Helen, we're going to have this out. The police have been round here questioning you. I know that. They told me. What did they ask? And why..." there was sudden blazing anger in him, "why are you so damn embarrassed? Now," he tossed his pen aside, "let's have it."

She looked as though she was going to cry. Her grey eyes filmed and one hand went nervously to the curve of one of the brown bangs against her smooth pink cheek.

"But, Mr. Winton..."

"Let's have it." He was suddenly so tired it was an effort to speak. "What happened?"

"They just wanted to know where you were on the second—last month I mean, Mr. Winton. Just that, and if I'd ever seen that woman round here and I haven't, Mr. Winton, so I could say so quite honestly."

"Woman! What woman?" He didn't realize the urgency in his voice till her eyes rounded in surprise.

She said nervously, "Irene Suttle they said her name was, when they showed me the photo and I..."

"Photo!" He couldn't bite back the explosion of sound. He saw the way she winced back against the chair, but all he could think of was a wild desire to see the photograph for himself, to bring what had been only a description alive to his eyes. "What did she look like?" he asked lamely at length.

"Oh...I don't know." Her cheeks reddened, "I

realize that's a silly statement, Mr. Winton, but honestly . . . she just didn't make an impression on me, if you can follow me? She was pale-looking in the photo and her hair was messy and her frock too long and she had big ugly sandals. It would have been taken at some picnic I think. There were two little boys and a baby with her, anyway."

"I see. And what did they say when you denied seeing her around here?"

"Nothing, Mr. Winton. They were very nice really." She spoke the words as though she was sure they would soothe him. He felt suddenly like laughing, only it wasn't funny at all. It was rather horrible that the police could suspect him of a violent crime but continue to be what she called "nice".

"And of course," he picked up the pen again, "you're all wondering what I've been up to."

Her tongue licked nervously at the pale lips that he had never seen coloured by lipstick. "Mr. Winton," she burst out at last, "this woman . . . I did see her name in the papers. It was something about . . ."

"I know."

"If there's anything I can do?" She spoke almost wistfully, but he shook his head.

"There's nothing, Helen. Except answer any questions the police put to you. Or to the rest of the staff. You might as well tell them that. For your information I never met that woman or had anything to do with her. Perhaps you'd get me that file on Coopers, would you?"

She rose quickly, then hesitated. "There's just one other thing, Mr. Winton. I've just remembered. It was rather silly really. They asked if you'd ever had a cat, but I said no, because you have Margold. Was that right?"

"The truth is always right." It was the only thing he could think of to say.

· · ·

156

Winton had a standing appointment on Wednesdays at the bowling alleys with Walter Parks. It was a relaxation he looked forward to, not only for the exercise and the quiet enjoyment in the game, but for Walter's company. It had been Victoria and Walter's small son who had introduced the two families and the friendship had grown slowly and steadily through the following two years. Like himself Walter had his roots in near poverty; like himself he had been blessed with luck and given an aptitude for hard work. The alley, along with its restaurant and pool, was Parks's. With Walter, unlike some of his other associates, there was no need for Winton to pretend he was something he wasn't. It was a relaxation of spirit as well as a relaxation of body and mind that he sought each late Wednesday afternoon.

But he sensed the change in Walter as soon as he changed into bowling shoes and hefted the first ball. He saw the sliding glance and felt suddenly sick.

Then the other man said simply, "George, the police have been round my place. Round the alley here, too."

"I see." He put the ball down and reached for cigarettes. The familiar action of lighting one was steadying. He squinted his gaze behind the lenses of his glasses at the curl of smoke, then asked, "What did they ask you?"

The answer was so unexpected that he choked on a lungful of smoke. When he had stopped coughing he blinked confusedly at the other man. "Did you say they asked you about Margold?"

"Uh huh." The other man rubbed one hand over the brushed back oiled black hair. "George," he looked steadily at the other man, "you in bad trouble? Has Margold attacked someone? I told you long ago you were a fool to train the brute like that, but you would have it . . ."

"Hold on." George shook his head. "You've stumped

me. Do you mean they told you Margold's attacked someone who's laid a complaint?"

"No. You must know that's not so. You weren't surprised when I told you the cops had been round." He
sounded impatient. "So why attempt surprise now?"

George held on to his patience by an effort. He suddenly
wanted to rage at the other man, even to strike at him, to
shake the whole story out of him. He said, after a long,
steadying breath, "Tell me just what they said."

"All right, if that's the way you want it." Walter picked
up one of the balls, hefting it, tossing it lightly as he
spoke, his gaze flickering towards the other alleys, looking,
George realized, to see if anyone was taking an undue
interest in the pair of them.

"They wanted to know how long you'd had the dog; if
you'd trained it as a watchdog and if so, how fierce was it?
Whether you kept it chained most of the time, or if it was
safe enough to roam around."

He spoke bluntly, "I told the truth. Going to let it bust
up our friendship, George? I didn't see how it would help to
lie, when anyone round here could say differently. They'd
wonder why I thought it necessary to give the truth a
run around, wouldn't they? They might even think you'd
put me up to it, which wouldn't help you a scrap. So I told
them the truth, that you've trained Margold to hold any
strangers who set foot on your place till you or Annie
come to look-see at who it is; that the dog's safe enough
to my mind, but you've trained it to attack on your
orders."

"Did you tell them," George asked almost absently, his
mind still trying to grabble with the idea of the police
being interested in the dog, "that you've warned me a
hundred times, if once, that one day Margold mightn't
wait for the order, and then I'd be in a mess?"

"No. George," there was suddenly relief in his square-jawed face and in the lighter tone of voice, "You're really puzzled, aren't you? You don't know why . . ."

"I told you I didn't. I expected the police to start asking round here, but not about the dog. It doesn't make sense."

"Does a question about a woman make sense then?"

"They asked that, too?"

"They showed me a photo; mentioned a name; asked if I'd heard of one, seen the original of the other. I said no to both." He shot out, "Who's this Irene Suttle, to come down to cases?"

"A woman I've never met. That's the truth, Walt, but the police think otherwise."

The other man's gaze was searching, then abruptly his big frame relaxed. He said lightly, "We've wasted enough time, haven't we? Get bowling, man."

.   .   .

Annie had washed her red hair and it hadn't dried. She was still in the garden, by the pool, when he came back in the sunset. The big Alsatian was close to her and its head lifted alertly as George came in sight, but it didn't move.

George flicked its ears and turned. He knew from the look of Annie, from a pallor that shouldn't be there, from a too-grimly tilted line of jaw, that the police had been to see her, and anger and tiredness were all mingled together again and the mental ease he had found in the game with Walter Parks at the alley were abruptly gone.

He knelt down beside her, putting his arms round her.

"Tell me, Annie," was all he could manage.

"It's funny," her fingers began to twist at the hair at the back of his head, "but they frightened me, yet they were all kiss-me-hand," she gave a little chuckle. "All lovey-dovey-coo, as Mrs. Gage'd say. They wanted to talk to her, too."

"What about?"

"Same as for me. They showed us a photo."

"You've seen it!" He almost shouted the words, and when she jerked away he asked urgently, "What did she really look like, Annie?"

"I'm no good at description," her tone was regretful. "Just pale. Wishy-washy I'd call her. Pale hair and pale dress and real unfashionable with it. What my dad would have called a feeble sort of soul."

"What did they ask you and Mrs. Gage?"

"Just if we'd seen her. Or heard her name. And then ... " her gaze flickered sideways.

"The dog," he said. "They asked about Margold."

"Yes," her touch on his hair tightened till he winced. "And I was scared. What'd they want to ask all those questions about Margold for? They even wanted to see him."

"I don't know," he admitted, "I don't know, Annie, and that's the sheer hell of it. What are they up to now?"

CHAPTER SIXTEEN

In the two days that followed he became used to the question, "You in bad trouble, George?" put in a dozen different ways, from friends and neighbours. Annie kept to the house and because they were both afraid of the child being questioned and upset, Vicky was kept indoors, too.

It brought an air of unreality into their lives. They found and tried to laugh at it, that they were talking in whispers and walking with softened steps as though all their words and movements were being watched and noted. They were two days that showed them only too clearly the unpleasantness and impossibility of normal life that lay ahead if the whole thing wasn't quickly cleared up.

Yet no one in the district seemed to know more than the fact that the police were asking questions about a woman and about the big dog. There had been no mention of the *Heron's* trip and of the accident at Comboroo. The two of them, when talk ran silent at last and they ceased for the moment to speculate uselessly on solutions to everything, came back to the same question—were the police deliberately trying to lead attention away from Comboroo and the accident? Deliberately concentrating on Margold, who had nothing to do with anything, in an effort to lull them into some sort of false security?

It was a question that nagged uselessly at them both.

And the police never came near them. Strangely enough, to George it was the goad that flicked the worst. It forced him, against his better judgment, into asking questions round the district himself, in an effort to find out what was happening.

He learned that way that the movements of his whole household for the night of Sunday, the twelfth of the previous month, had been in question. It added another puzzle to the mountain of speculation and puzzlement and fear that gnawed at them both.

"Do *you* remember what we did?" they whispered in the darkness to each other.

They had finally worked it out that as usual, Nanny and Mrs. Gage had had their Sunday afternoon and evening off and Annie herself had taken Victoria to a children's party and returned about six. Vicky had been sent early to bed after all the excitement and he and Annie had watched television, eaten off trays, washed the dishes together because Annie hated them being stacked overnight, and then gone to bed.

"But why are we getting in a tizzy about it anyway?" Annie whispered against his side. "It was just another Sunday. There wasn't anything special."

He said that, when the police came back on the following day and asked him about that Sunday that now seemed quite remote to him because of all that had happened since.

Gregor asked, "Does the housekeeper have a key? And the nurse?" At George's nod, he demanded, "Did you speak to them when they came back?"

"Not that I remember." Then he amended, "I think Annie did go out to speak to the baby's nurse. Vicky had had too much to eat at the party and she was grizzling and playing up when we put her to bed. I think Annie went to tell the nurse so and ask her to listen in case Vicky woke."

"You didn't appear yourself?"

"No." In sudden impatience he burst out, "What's all this in aid of? Why didn't you ask me this in the first place, instead of going behind my back?" He knew rage was taking over from common-sense again, but he didn't care. "I've known for days you were going to ask this. I found out from gossip that people hardly even known to me were being questioned about my private doings. Do you think that . . ."

"When I ask you a question, Mr. Winton," Gregor gave back almost gently, "you don't seem inclined to tell me the truth. To return to this particular night—there's only your wife's word that you were home. Is that right?"

"If you put it that way, yes, but Annie has no reason for lying about it. Neither have I."

"That, Mr. Winton, happens to be the last time Miss Suttle was known to be in her house."

George knew his body had gone stiff with shock. He was going to speak; going to blurt out that the woman had been alive on the Monday night, when she had gone baby-sitting for Kiley, when he remembered he wasn't supposed to know anything about her. He sat there, trying to decide whether to say Kiley had mentioned it, or whether Kiley would deny it.

Then Gregor said, "She was seen late on Sunday by someone passing the house. She hasn't been seen, or heard of, since."

His voice croaked into the silence, "I thought I was suspected of taking her somewhere on the morning of the seventeenth? There's quite a gap, there, isn't there?"

A little flicker of triumph showed in Gregor's brown eyes. "But there was bad weather, Mr. Winton. From Friday the tenth right up to the night of the sixteenth and morning of the seventeenth there'd been storms and the sea had been extremely rough. It would have been fool-hardy to take out a small boat along this coastline."

Gregor looked down at his hands as though fascinated by the dark hairs growing on their leanness. "Milk was left for her on the Monday morning. Someone took that in. And bread. That went, too. Tuesday there was a note about the milk. The baker only called every second day. He wasn't there Tuesday morning."

George managed, "Obviously she was there Monday morning. She . . ."

"No. No one saw her. There were no light in her house that evening."

His voice was too high, too excited, when he burst out, "She often baby-sat for Evan Kiley. She was probably in his house that night. She . . ."

"So you *had* heard of Miss Suttle before we asked you about her, Mr. Winton?"

He hesitated. The hot air seemed almost suffocating as the seconds ticked by. Then he said, "No. I've seen Kiley since. We had . . . business to discuss. We naturally mentioned this affair, and he said she'd often baby-sat with his small son. He said . . ."

"She didn't that Monday night, according to Kiley. He wanted her to do so because his housekeeper had walked out on him and his wife wasn't there, so he went round, but he could get no answer to his knocking and ringing, though she hardly ever went out. Retiring, is how everyone described her, Mr. Winton. Shy and retiring and a stay-at-home. But she wasn't at home on Monday, and we can't find anyone for whom she baby-sat that night. She occasionally sat with the children of another household in Comboroo. Nowhere else that we can discover. And there were no lights in her house. Kiley had to send for a cousin of his wife's family to come and care for his boy. That relative took the lad to his own home that night, so Miss Suttle wasn't in the Kiley house."

He sat there turning Kiley's story over in thought. He could see how the younger man must have reasoned. If he had admitted to Irene being in the house, he would have admitted to being the last person to see her. He had wanted to keep clear, in his own words, of being concerned in any way. So Kiley had lied again. He wondered, sitting in silence, waiting for whatever else was coming, if the lie would make his own position worse, or better, or have no effect at all.

Gregor went on, "You say you were at Ireland's Bay on the second of last month. Can you prove that?"

He tried desperately to raise features, voices, from memory, but in the end he had to say lamely, "I doubt it. I was on my own. Deliberately so. I wanted to see over the place without distracting talk."

"Then let me ask you something else, Mr. Winton. You have a dog, haven't you?"

"Yes. And I know you've been asking questions about it all over the district," George challenged. "Why?"

Gregor didn't answer. Instead he asked, "You've trained it to challenge anyone who comes to this house, haven't you?"

"Yes. There've been a lot of thefts round this way. Englebert," his gaze slid sideways towards the silent policeman, "must know that."

He thought that Englebert looked embarrassed and ill-at-ease. He felt slightly sick when the policeman's gaze turned away from his own. It was a reminder of the past few days. He wondered in despair how long it was going to go on—the sliding gaze, the whispers, the questioning that seemed with every answer to drag him deeper into trouble.

"You've trained it to attack, on your orders, haven't you?"

"Yes."

"Did you ever take the dog with you when visiting Miss Suttle?"

George felt a surge of amusement bubbling deep in his throat. He said lightly, "That sort of trick won't help you, because I never visited her."

"Then how does it come about there are the marks of a dog's paws on her kitchen floor, Mr. Winton? She didn't have a dog. This must have been a big dog—a very big dog, Mr. Winton. Like your Margold. And its feet were muddy. On Sunday the twelfth at night, Mr. Winton, there was rain."

He knew that sick rememberance must be showing on his face and that the two policemen were going to jump to the wrong conclusions about it. He could remember so clearly that night when he and Annie had gone to the mountain and he had called Margold to his side, on seeing that flickering torchlight, and gone into the dark silent house.

He said thickly at last, "There are thousands of dogs in . . ."

"Not on the mountain at Comboroo, Mr. Winton. The only one that way is a small puppy, but there was a very big dog in her house at one time and you wouldn't think she would leave the muddy prints there on the floor for very long, would you?"

He said without thinking, "She was a bit of a slut and left things . . ." then he stopped.

There was no change of expression in Gregor's face. He might not have noticed that the other man had made a disastrous slip and had given evidence of knowledge about the missing woman.

George tried to retrieve the slip. He said urgently, "Kiley and I discussed her, of course, and he told me quite a bit about her."

"You're sure you never visited her, Mr. Winton?"

"I never visited her," he said hopelessly. It seemed so ridiculous that the truth was so simple and yet he couldn't say it. Then he demanded, "If I had why should I take the dog anyway?"

"You've trained that dog to attack, Mr. Winton. You've admitted it."

It was unbearable to sit there and listen to the slow unfolding of suspicion and evidence and conjecture. He challenged, "You think I took the dog and ordered it to attack her and then when she was held down . . . I killed her. Is that it?"

Gregor didn't answer for a moment, then he said quietly, "Accidents happen, Mr. Winton. If there was a quarrel in which Miss Suttle lost her temper and struck at you, your dog might have protected you, mightn't it, and attacked her in turn and seriously injured her."

George shook his head. He wondered if the police actually thought that was what had happened, or whether they were more inclined to think he had taken the dog deliberately and ordered it to attack and kill. He knew that Gregor was hoping he would admit to the lesser crime, to accidental death, to avoid the agony of an endlessly drawn out investigation and perhaps a graver charge.

He said at last, "It's quite untrue. I never visited her. Margold didn't attack her."

"Then where is she now, Mr. Winton?"

. . .

They can't prove anything.

The words were a talisman that they clung to through the dragging hours of the next few days. In spite of the common-sense that told him Kiley was unlikely now to alter his story of not seeing Irene Suttle that Monday, Winton had phoned the other man again at the Sydney press office. He had wanted to urge him to alter the story; to say that Miriam's cousin perhaps, had seen the woman that Monday night leaving her house, because for that night he had the perfect answer — he and Annie had been present at a meeting all evening, not like Sunday, when there was only Annie's sole word that he had been safely at home.

But Kiley, as soon as he had recognized the voice speaking to him, had put down the receiver. He hadn't banged it down in anger. There had been just a gentle click in George's ear and then silence.

"But they can't prove anything," Annie said hopefully.

"No, they can't prove anything." He clung desperately to the talisman of the words.

It was suddenly as though they were islanded and stranded alone with companionship in sight but separated from them by a gap that was just too great for them to bridge, because the phone rang and the mail came and one by one long-standing appointments for them both for picnics and parties, for meetings and theatre going, were all cancelled.

Annie tried to laugh at what she called the sudden epidemic of relative troubles. "If grannies aren't dying, love," she smiled up at him from one morning's batch of mail, "then a second cousin and nineteen offspring have landed without warning; aunts are miscarrying, uncles falling off chimneys, and nephews being bitten by snakes."

But even her smiles and attempted laughter had vanished when even Victoria's life became as limited as their own. Two parties became suddenly barred to her on feeble excuses and one expected invitation was never given at all.

Annie simply showed him the letters cancelling the party invitations. Neither of them said anything, but on to the burdens of thought already with him, came the weight of the child's disappointment, and the sight of deepening circles under Annie's blue eyes.

Jacobs had told his story of the *Heron's* trip out to sea. They knew that, because slowly the gossip and speculation filtered back to them through the housekeeper and the child's nurse. They knew the district had put together the questions about the woman in the photograph, and the dog and the long heavy bundle that had been taken out to sea and had turned them into monstrous imaginings.

At first they had said, "It'll stop soon. Like a bushfire, there'll be nothing left to gossip over and keep the flames burning," but it didn't work out that way. It seemed that each day brought a new item to whisper about; stories started heaven knew where of himself and Annie at loggerheads; of a dog's fierce barking in the dead of night on the deserted beach; of himself coming back that dawn of the *Heron's* trip, white-faced and shaking. With each repetition the stories seemed to grow detail by tiny detail and all they could do was face each other and say, "They can't prove anything," and try to find consolation in it.

He thought, when the police came that day, that at last it would stop—that the fierce fire of gossip would be damped down and finished with.

He said slowly, almost unbelievingly, hardly daring to touch the words with his tongue for fear of proving them false, "You mean you've proved I couldn't have been in Comboroo that day of the accident?"

"That's right, Mr. Winton," Gregor agreed. "You weren't near the place at all."

He had expected some embarrassment in the brown eyes, some apology in the voice, but it hadn't been there, and in sudden rage he had burst out, "It's taken you long enough to find it out! I told you over and over again I wasn't there. I told you I went to the north—to Ireland's Bay—looking over land there. I told you . . ."

"We couldn't accept your word alone, Mr. Winton."

There was still no apology or embarrassment about Gregor's smooth reply. "And it's been hard to find anyone who saw you that day. We have the word of two timber men who saw you though. They'd seen you about a few weeks before and had been speculating about what you intended to do with the land you were looking over. They remembered you and the times you came."

He drew a deep breath. "So it's all over. You can see now that . . ."

But of course it wasn't. In the gratitude and delight of

169

relief at having one of his statements accepted he had completely forgotten all the rest of the endless questions he had answered; forgotten the questions that had been asked and answered by others, and of them.

"I see you could have had nothing to do with that accident, Mr. Winton," Gregor bowed to that admission. "Presumably Miss Suttle told the truth so far as she knew it. We can't *know* though. She still hasn't come forward. No one has seen her. Or heard from her. She disappeared on the night of the twelfth and proving you had nothing to do with that accident, Mr. Winton, doesn't do anything towards clearing you of the facts that you wrote the note attached to her door; that you had some of her possessions in your car; that paw marks that are certainly your dog's were in her house; that you disposed of her cat. Mr. Winton, where is she now?"

He had lost his temper and common-sense in a violent explosion as he had snapped out, "If you're sure now she didn't have something on me I wanted to hide, there's only one thing you can be thinking—that I've been playing the fool with her and was tired of her and either by accident or design I'm now rid of her. You think, don't you, that she's dead and that I took her body out to sea in the *Heron* and threw her overboard. It's what all the district is chewing over and it's impossible. Surely to heaven you can see that!" he cried desperately. "Why should I have wanted to bother with a grubby little slut of a woman like Irene Suttle who ..."

It was the strange look on Englebert's face that stopped his tirade. He stopped, feeling that he had run some difficult race, only to find that he had gone backwards, in the wrong direction.

Gregor shook his head. "Isn't it strange, Mr. Winton, that you seem to know so much about her? When you say you never met. When you *say* you didn't."

CHAPTER SEVENTEEN

IT had been three weeks of a purgatory that should have inured him to the sideways slide of caught glances, but when Walter Parks came to the house that Sunday and he saw the way the big man's gaze slid away from his own he said tightly, "Walt, either look me in the face or get out of the house!"

The big man shook his head. "Losing your temper isn't going to help, George. Alright, I'm not looking you in the face. It's because I don't like seeing the way you've changed. You're a lot harder and a lot older and a damn sight more difficult to get on with than you were a few weeks ago. That's part of the reason. And I'm not looking at you because I'm embarrassed at what I've got to tell you now. And to finish it I'm not looking at you because I don't want to see your expression when I tell it."

George gazed at him silently for a moment, then without a word he turned on his heel and led the way inside to the sitting-room. He took the black leather chair himself and nodded to the yellow one opposite.

When the big man was seated, George asked, "What is it? Gossip you think I ought to know? We know what's being said, or most of it. Annie and I haven't much pride these days." He was conscious of the bitter defiance in his voice, but he didn't try to alter it. "We pump the help. They don't like it and neither do we, and we're expecting them to walk out soon, but pumping them keeps us abreast of what the milkman and the baker and the butcher and the candlestick-maker get from the rest of their customers, embroider it a little and pass it on. Annie and I've found out a lot in the past few weeks, Walt—including how dirty the human mind can think."

He saw the big shoulders move in a little shrug and went on with the same bitter defiance, "The choicest gossip seems to be I made two women pregnant at the same time and now I've got rid of one."

"Don Juan Winton." It was more a rumble of sound than clear-cut words.

"A week ago I might have laughed, Walt. Now I can't. What did you come about?"

"Josie."

He hadn't expected that and the answer was so unexpected that he abruptly chuckled. He said lightly, "After letting me blow my top you calmly say it's your teenage daughter you want to talk about. Did you think it ... what do they call it? ... therapy? ... to let me lift the lid on things?"

"No. Josie," he hesitated after speaking the name of his thirteen-year-old daughter again, "sometimes takes Tim and Victoria down to the park to play on the swings and so on down there."

"What of it?"

"A while back she was doing just that. The kids were in with a group that afternoon playing some sort of ball game. Josie sat down to watch, ready to stick her oar in if they got out of hand. After a bit a woman sat down beside her. She started talking to Josie. Josie didn't see any harm in it, or in gossiping to the woman about Vicky and Annie and yourself."

"Do you mean you've found out now the woman was from the press?" He felt desperately sick, though it was something he had been waiting for. He and Annie had seen, when the rumours had spread about Victoria's disappearance, how ruthless and patient the press people had been. He had expected them to come prowling around, picking up a detail here and a fact there, ready for a possible arrest, for the possible breaking of a story about Irene Suttle or himself.

"No. This was some time ago, George. About three or four months back."

"Then what . . ."

"Josie says the woman was the woman in that photograph the police have been showing around."

He became conscious of Vicky shrieking with delight somewhere outside. And somewhere someone was using a power mower. They were the only sounds.

He wasn't angry. There was only a feeling of sadness, that even a child had joined in the spite and gossip.

He said almost gently, "You know that can't be true, Walt."

"Don't think I took her word, just like that," was the blunt response. "I had her near to tears before I was finished, but Laura and I were both sure when we'd sucked her dry. She believes it, George. She's dead certain the woman who questioned her about you that day was the woman in that photo."

He still didn't sound, or feel, angry. He said with the same gentleness, "It's not true, Walt. I haven't seen the photo, but from what I've heard there's nothing outstanding, easily rememberable about . . ."

"*I've* seen it. It's clear enough. You could pick someone out from it if you saw them around."

"The point is it's four months ago and Josie wouldn't have paid much attention to the woman, I expect, and . . ."

"She says she did, because after a while she got uncomfortable about the questions and clammed up. She says she remembers her quite well and it's the same woman as in the photo."

"It's not possible, Walt. I don't think she'd lie—she' old enough to know what's being said and to know she might get me into worse trouble. I don't believe she'd try to do that. Or would she? Kids of her age . . ."

"It's no good, George. Trying to smear Josie won't help and I'm not biting your head off with saying that. It's just stating facts. Josie's a placid sort of kid, she's bright and has a good memory and she's not given to lying. Her teachers and anyone round here would say so. And to top it she likes you. So she wouldn't lie. She told me about it because the police came to us again. Josie was home and they showed her the photo. She didn't say anything to them. She told me and Laura afterwards. But she's certain, George."

"It's not true. It's impossible. She's mistaken, or she's lying."

He knew a sense of complete loss. He didn't know what was going to happen, whether the big man was going to walk out and go to the police, or stay silent, but he knew their friendship was finished. Because Walter Parks believed his daughter.

The big man stood up. He said slowly, "If that's all you've got to say, George, it's useless me hanging around. Isn't it?"

"I guess so. Walt," he said in sudden urgency as the other man started to move towards the door, "would Josie come down to talk to me? And Annie?"

For a minute the other man hesitated, then he shook his head. "There's no point in that. She's told her story to me and Laura."

He got his tongue round the question finally. It came out jerkily as the big man stepped through the door.

"Are you going to the police, Walt?"

"I think so." He turned back. "It's this way, George— this thing's been preying on Josie's mind for days. She can't sleep and she can't eat and she's making herself sick. It's better, both Laura and I think, for her to tell it to the

174

police and have done with it. It's Josie I've got to think of, George. And . . . if there's nothing in it, like you say . . . they can't prove anything against you, can they?"

"No."

But the talisman seemed suddenly very frail as he slowly nodded, "they can't prove anything, Walt. Nothing at all."

⋅   ⋅   ⋅

He had expected fear from Annie, and rage, but there was only a despair to equal his own and an acceptance of the blue as though fear was so tightly confined in them that there was simply no room for any more.

"She's a liar," Annie repeated the words dully over and over again. "She's a liar."

"Walter's convinced she's telling the truth," he told her flatly. "He's frightened for her. He's scared what effect this might have on her—the publicity, the questioning, the whole filthy mess of it. He told me he and Laura nearly reduced her to tears before he was sure she was telling the truth as she saw it—they made quite certain."

"I bet. I bet she was near to tears, George love, because she's a liar. Oh she never meant to cause trouble at the start. I'll lay you anything on that. She just did it to make herself feel big. Kids do. And then it all ran away with her. They took it for gospel and were probably so scared and funny about it, that she took fright. She wasn't game to admit she lied. She's stuck with it now and that makes it worse because a frightened kid's like nothing else on earth." Her hand sought his in desperate clutch. "They're stubborn and cunning and quick as a knife at covering up for themselves and you can't bully them like you would an adult. She's stuck with it and so are we."

"But they can't prove anything."

She didn't answer. Her blue eyes were blank. He was

sure she was looking ahead, into the wilderness that lay waiting for them; a wilderness in which their only companion was going to be gossip.

He said desperately, "We'll go away, Annie. Even if they won't let me go, you and Victoria can."

"No. I'm staying. If I run it'll be worse. They'll say . . . that world peopled with *they* . . ." a ghost of her old smile touched her mouth, "that I've found you out at last and beaten it before you take me out in the *Heron*, too. Remember I'm supposed to own half all your goods, George love? Remember you made me a partner in everything? *They'll* say you might have got rid of me if I'd stayed, for fear of me lighting out with my half of everything. They'll say . . ."

"Annie, stop it," he pleaded.

"It's not fair," her voice whispered against his chest, "we did nothing wrong. We don't deserve . . ."

"We did. We kept silence about Vicky going. If we hadn't, Kiley wouldn't have come to me like that and I wouldn't have been drawn into the mess. If we'd only let the whole story out when she came back . . ."

"If, if, if," she mocked gently. "You sound like a popping gas stove, George love. If, if, if . . . oh let's forget it. Please!"

•   •   •

He knew he had behaved like a fool, but there had been no room in thought for anything but the urgent desire to see Josie and talk to her face to face and get the truth. He had lied to Annie, because he didn't want her to know where he was going and try to persuade him against going.

The black sky was smudged to greyness where the orange moon was coming up, blotting out starlight, when he turned into the Parks' driveway. He could see the colour of the scarlet poinsettias coming slowly to life again in the moonlight as he went up to the door and knocked — the side door, because that was always where he and Annie went—never to the front.

Walter called the front one the visitors' door and the side one the friends' door, but there was nothing friendly about his expression when he saw who had knocked.

He said, quite simply, "George, go away, please."

"No. I'm not going till I've seen Josie. I won't hurt her and I won't frighten her. You can see to that for yourself. All I want to do is hear her story and I think I'm entitled to ask that much."

He thought there was going to be a blunt refusal, then the other man stood aside. He said, "Laura's gone over to her mother's. The old lady isn't so good. Tim's in bed and I was just seeing Josie off."

"Have you told . . .?" He couldn't keep the anxiety out of his voice.

"I saw them. I only got home an hour back. They're interviewing Josie in the morning. She seems easier in her mind now the decision what to do's been made for her, but I was getting a drink ready for her, with some stuff in it, so she'll sleep."

He nodded to the open door of the sitting-room. "Go on in. I'll get Josie."

But it was a long time before he came back. George wondered with a calmness that surprised him, if the big man mightn't even be using the time to summon the police—if he wasn't telling them of his visitor and asking what he should do.

But when the big man came back he said, half impatiently, "The blasted milk boiled over while I was answering the door. Josie's in the bathroom. I've told her to hurry out. Want a drink?"

George shook his head. There seemed nothing more to

say, and he felt the wearying sickness creep over him again that came with every fresh assault to friendship and dignity and privacy. Normally he and George would have been lost in eager conversation within seconds of sitting down beside each other. Now there was only silence between them.

Then abruptly he was conscious of being watched. He looked up and saw Josie in the doorway of the room. Like her mother she was slim and dark, with straight black hair that she wore in a thick long fringe that reached almost to her beautifully arched dark brows. He had often looked at her in appreciation, thinking that in a few years she would be beautiful. Now she looked a mess. Her face seemed swollen and her grey eyes had receded into puffed-up reddened lids. Even her mouth seemed swollen with the violence of tears.

He was suddenly ashamed and contrite because that violence had been on his own account.

He said gently, "Josie . . ."

"Mr. Winton," her voice was thin and high, "I told the truth. I did see that lady in the photo and she spoke to me in the park that day just like I told dad and like he's told the police. I wouldn't say if it wasn't true. I just wouldn't."

"I believe you, Josie." He tried to smile at her. "Where I think you're wrong is in thinking it's the same woman, because it couldn't possibly be."

"It was. It's not her looks so much." She was suddenly eager to convince him, to make him understand. She crossed to him, quite unselfconscious in the white short pyjamas that showed the lines of her slim body, "It was her dress mostly. It was the same one, you see and it was such an awful messy looking thing—real long, and the sleeves were miles too wide and it had those huge spots all over it. It was just like that day in the park. It was the dress I remember really more than her face."

He was suddenly lost in memory, smelling the bitter smell of too long wearing as he took the cream dress with the big pale blue spots from its hanger and folded it clumsily into the case.

"What did she ask you, Josie?" he demanded.

"Well . . . things. I just thought at first it was Vicky she was interested in. Right at first, but then . . . she got sort of nosey and I clammed up. She wanted to know if you were having another baby maybe and I said . . ." she faltered, then admitted, "I said no, but Mrs. Winton was just hoping and hoping there would be one soon. I heard," she admitted awkwardly, "Mum and Mrs. Winton talking about it."

He smiled at her and faintly encouraged she went on, "She wanted to know what sort of person you were and what Mrs. Winton was like—if you were kind and . . . oh, it was sort of silly really. And she asked about your boat—where it was, what it was like, things like that."

She stood on one leg, uneasily, as he remained silent. Then she said heavily, "I told the truth, Mr. Winton." Then abruptly she turned and ran out of the room.

"Going to blub again," Walter said grimly.

George stood up. He asked diffidently, "How does Laura feel about . . ."

"Same as me. We're sorry and we're puzzled and we're worried and we're just plain wild at your attitude, George."

"All right." He hesitated, then finally turned away. He gave back lamely over his shoulder, "Goodnight, Walt, and thanks. You'd better take that drink in to Josie."

"Have to make some more now," the big man said slowly as though it helped to talk of trivial things. He went on talking as he followed his visitor down the hall and out on to the little side porch. "The last lot went everyway-which-place over the stove, and I'll have to clean that up before Laura gets a sight of it or I'll spend the night howl-ing in the dog-house." He stopped. He said suddenly, "Goodbye, George," and then he turned away and the door closed.

It was that that went with George down the path. Not the memory of Josie's reddened eyes; or the thought of the gossip and the morning and the fear and distrust of the past weeks—just a simple goodbye. Not goodnight. Not a friendly farewell. But a cold goodbye.

CHAPTER EIGHTEEN

He lay awake, trying not to move because Annie had finally dropped off at his side. He hadn't told her anything about his trip to see Josie. He had said only that his walk had done him good and he was ready for bed. He hadn't wanted to say more. He had wanted time, desperately, to think, but even in the quiet, warm darkness there had been so many things that clamoured endlessly for his attention that he felt his body tensing in a fury of frustrated creativeness.

It was nearly dawn when he slipped his arm from around Annie and pulled himself upright. Annie stirred slightly and he said her name, gently touching her. She came back to consciousness slowly, then abruptly there was alertness in the moon-silvered face upraised to his.

She asked, "What is it? What happened?" and he could see the pulse-beat of panic throbbing in the side of her white neck.

He said, "Annie, I want to talk. I don't know if I'm crazy or what, but I've got to talk to you."

"Go ahead, love." She might have been speaking to Victoria, soothingly, gentling away some nightmare out of the darkness.

The words were there; had been in his thoughts for over an hour; but suddenly he didn't want to speak them, because he was afraid that she would listen and shatter the words and the thoughts into fragments.

Reluctantly he said at last, "Annie, Kiley's story is impossible."

"Which one?" she asked tiredly. "That man's..."

"The story he told us that first morning, when we first set eyes on him. Please listen, Annie."

"I'm not interrupting," she pointed out.

"It's impossible. Remember how he told us the gas burner on the stove was full on? If there'd been something on the stove it wouldn't have taken so long to boil over. Now would it? And how long would it take, on the other hand, for a woman to be interrupted in her heating of something, to talk to someone, to argue, to agree to being bound up, to be bound up, for someone to go away and leave her? It'd take a long time, Annie. Wouldn't it? Whatever was on the stove would have boiled over long before that second person went away.

"Last night—at Walter's—I was there, Annie—it only took the time of him answering the door to me for the milk on his stove to boil right over. Do you see what I'm getting at? It's wrong, Annie. The story doesn't add up. If it only took minutes last night for milk on Walter's stove to boil over, why did it take so long that other night, when Kiley's boy is supposed to have gone?

"It didn't dawn on me at first and then . . . I kept going over and over Josie's story and last night and then I remembered the milk and Kiley's story and . . . it was there in front of me—a lie—something that couldn't have been as Kiley had said. And when I kept thinking . . . don't you see, Annie," he pressed desperately, "that his story— the rest of it—hinges on it having happened as he claims— on something boiling over by accident, by . . ."

His voice trailed away. He waited for her to say something, but she went on lying quite still. At last she asked, "Do you mean, you think it was a lie because he killed her. Kiley? Deliberately? Or in a fight, maybe? And he tried to cover up by throwing the blame . . . but that's impossible!"

"No. Annie, we've been fools. That whole story—I remember you saying it seemed unreal. You sensed it then. And I remember I felt once I was a ham actor on some stage set and it wasn't real to me, then, but it was all so plausible and we were both sick with the thought we were partly responsible. Kiley kept goading us, reminding us we were to blame, because we'd kept silent."

"What are you getting at?" her voice had sharpened. He could see the pulse-beat in her throat was slowing. He wondered, in sudden desperation, if she wasn't going to listen any more, or listen with only half an ear, while she whispered soothing words, refusing to believe him.

He said urgently, "Annie, what would have happened if the Kiley pair had come to us and simply said their son was gone and they'd had a demand for money? Would you have believed it? Knowing Kiley was a pressman? After the way they'd hounded us for the story?"

She said instantly, "No. I wouldn't have, but . . ."

"Yes, *but* . . . but someone was dead. It made it all instantly plausible, didn't it? Someone was dead and we were made to feel it was our fault for not telling the police once we had Vicky safely back. We'd made it possible for another kidnapping to happen; for a woman to die; and we weren't allowed to forget those points."

"But . . . what are you getting at?" She sounded irritable now. "She was dead and there's no bucking that, but . . ."

"But what if she wasn't dead, Annie? What if the story was all a lie?"

"You mean . . . oh I don't know *what* you mean!"

"Then I'll start where I think it started—with us keeping quiet. Kiley heard those rumours and laid a plot. The basis of it was his son was to be kidnapped . . . or apparently so. But we had to be made to believe in the story. So someone had to die. Annie, I don't think there ever was a woman called Irene Suttle. No wait . . . look at it this way.

Miriam Kiley's an actress and for six months she wasn't seen in Comboroo. What if, in those months, she was really playing a part—the part of Irene Suttle?

"Yes, I know—they told us Irene Suttle arrived next door to them a month before Miriam went, but would it have been too hard for Miriam to have been herself and Irene for that one month? Remember, Irene kept to herself. And Miriam was supposed to be deciding to leave her husband and son. She could have avoided her friends—it would have been an excuse, too, for her not being friendly to a newcomer—for the two women not to have to be seen together. Miriam was keeping to herself—sulking if you like. She wasn't interested in Comboroo any more. Or in a new neighbour. And Irene was shy and quiet and didn't know anyone. Miriam could easily have made a few appearances in the town as herself, and a few others as the newcomer, Irene Suttle. And then Miriam went. And only Irene was left.

"And don't you see how ghostly Irene Suttle's life appears to be? She came from nowhere. None of her old friends have come forward mentioning her, or we'd have heard. Think carefully about Miriam Kiley, Annie—she's not a type who's easy to remember. She could easily alter her appearance—different make-up, a wig, different clothes—she'd be easy to alter.

"And then Irene . . . she avoided people, except for Kiley and for baby-sitting for one other family. She didn't make friends. She apparently had an income of her own because she didn't work. But where did it come from? No one's said. The only people who knew her at all well were supposedly Kiley and his wife.

"Annie, she never existed. I'm certain of it. She was brought to life and brought to death to fool you and me. If you look at that business of the gassing and know it's a lie, there has to be a reason for the lie. At first I thought as you did—what if he killed her? Deliberately? Maybe because he'd played the fool with her and she'd become tiresome, threatening . . . and he saw a chance of getting rid of her and then . . . but there are too many points to cover. How could he know Miriam would go on faking the kidnapping when she knew and not just send Robin back? How did he know she wouldn't say she'd looked at the stove before she left and there'd been nothing on it and so cast suspicion on him? How did he know he was going to be able to get rid of the body the way he did . . . it all kept going round and round and round in my head and all I could think of was 'It's a lie.' The lot of it. It's a fraud. Fraud, Annie."

When she didn't answer he pressed on, "We had to believe in her and in her death, but in the end she had to be disposed of some way without me going to the police. So the story of Miriam being the cause of her death was worked out and we fell for that, too. I was too cowardly to look at the 'body'—I never thought the whole story was a fraud. Kiley counted on me being a coward, and he'd made her so real, Annie. He described her; there were the things in her house right down to worn clothes, her name in books. There was her cat, even the final touch of that cake coming after her death. She seemed real.

"But she wasn't. I don't believe it.

"She was here, Annie, asking questions about us and about our boat—everything she could get on us—months ago. Why? We'd never had any connection with her at all. I think it was Miriam who asked those questions to get all the background she could about us. Kiley wouldn't have come. Or Miriam as herself. Because they were going to come later on, to spin us that story and they might have been recognized as the ones who asked questions about us before—someone they questioned might have told us about it and described them to us.

"Annie, I'm sure of it." He was trying to make her as certain as himself, but there was no response from her still rigid body. "How did Kiley know he could get away with saying she wasn't in his house that Monday? Someone might have called he didn't know about, or she could have told someone, if his story was true. But it wasn't. He was sure no one would call him a liar.

"As for Robin—I don't think there's even a cousin, Annie. I think, if we search, we'll find a children's home somewhere who took in a little boy—Robin Kiley, Annie —while his mother was 'sick'. Any excuse would do. Who'd question it, so long as the bill was paid?"

"Do you mean," there was a slow coming to life, and to rage, through her whole body and voice. He could feel it and hear it, "that he did all that—to get our story out of us? To ... get ... a scoop, don't they call it? All that and let us ..."

"I doubt if anyone would have thought the best scoop in the world worth it, Annie, and he would simply have admitted it later and have the world laugh at us. No, you've forgotten something. He got nineteen thousand one hundred and fifty pounds out of you and me. And even the amount, his insistence on that sum and not a round sum like twenty thousand—it made it seem more plausible than ever, didn't it?"

"But you had the land, or isn't that his at all?" she demanded sharply.

"It's his, I'll grant you. But it's worthless. If I'm right. How did that story of Kiley's land start? In the press. And Kiley's a pressman. A hint there, an item here, a paragraph there and there's a story. It would have been so easy for him and it didn't matter a jot that it was promptly denied by the government. That's happened before. If we'd had time to think; if we hadn't been goaded by conscience the whole time we might have thought of fraud.

I don't know. Perhaps. Perhaps not. But the story was there and his son was gone and it seemed so plausible it should happen after a press story about him. It had happened to us and to the Griffen couple. It's fraud, Annie. I'm sure of it. Fraud for nineteen thousand odd pounds. There's nothing else to believe if you think Josie's telling the truth, and I do. Irene Suttle—a woman dressed as someone called that—was here months ago asking questions about us. Why? And why, on that night in Comboroo, did something on a stove take an impossible time to boil over?"

There suddenly wasn't even anger in him any more. There was only tiredness. "And he wouldn't admit to it. He left us to sweat all this out. He wouldn't and couldn't admit to the truth."

CHAPTER NINETEEN

HE had simply told Kiley, in that phone call to the other man, that he had to see him; that something had happened that involved him and Miriam as well as the Wintons. There had been a silence so long that the exchange had broken in with the warning signal of minutes speeding by, then Kiley had said slowly, "I think you're fooling me. You'd better not. But all right. Come, if you really have to."

There was sunshine that day, as hard and as brilliant as on the northern coast, but the sky was a softer blue. It was mirrored in the water of the fountains and the Pool of Reflection as George walked towards the memorial, his gaze on the tall figure already standing there.

Kiley turned to face him. His hands were in his pockets. He looked relaxed, but his freckled face showed no welcome.

He said shortly, "Well, what's your story?"

"Fraud."

He saw the pale eyes narrow, but Kiley didn't speak, and he didn't break the silence himself. He knew that Kiley was trying to force him into speech; that he considered himself the stronger of the pair of them; that he had thought that all along.

The remembrance of that taunt, "You're a bunny, George," was there with him as the silence went on. Then Kiley moved slightly. He said, squinting his eyes against the sun, "Listen, you got me here on some tale of me being involved in a new mess. Hadn't you better tell me what it's all about?"

"Fraud," George said again.

"What fraud?"

"Yours. And Miriam's. It's taken a long time and I've been a fool, but I've worked it out because a girl—a thirteen-year-old girl, Kiley—spoke out. She saw Irene Suttle four months ago and answered questions the woman put to her. Questions about me, Kiley. About my boat. That boat was important to your plan, wasn't it? If I hadn't had one maybe I'd have had to help you dig a grave for Irene Suttle, mightn't I? There were questions about my household, my wife, myself. And there was no reason—I didn't know her, she wasn't supposed to know me—unless my guess is the right one."

"Tell me what you've worked out," Kiley said quite equably.

He listened almost abstractedly, then at the last he suddenly grinned. "Congratulations, George," his voice was soft.

"That's how it was, wasn't it?" George demanded. "You found out all about us and you worked on our fears and our conscience and you made it sound very plausible. Nineteen thousand one hundred and fifty. It seemed so genuine."

Kiley nodded. "I thought myself that was the perfect touch."

"I'll tell you another—Miriam calling me at dawn and babbling about the way she wouldn't be able to bear being shut up—a whole heap on lines like that. I was to remember that, wasn't I, when the point was raised of telling the police and letting her go to prison.

"And I'll tell you another—you didn't ask outright for the money. You wanted me to stand guarantee with the bank, but you were pretty certain I'd offer the money outright, weren't you? To salve my conscience." The words were bitter on his tongue when he remembered the cold sweating agony of those few days. "What would you have done though, if I hadn't offered? Accepted the guarantee and left me to find the money to repay the bank eventually?"

When Kiley didn't answer he went on rapidly, "You never gave me time for thinking. You got me waiting at those lockers just to keep me occupied, didn't you? To make it seem more plausible—the distracted father working things out—trying to get a lead onto his son's kidnappers. You goaded me. You quarrelled with me. Even afterwards you accused me of witholding a decent price for the land. You put me on the defensive. What," he shot out, "would you have done if I'd demanded the money back after we'd disposed of the 'body'?"

"Lit out," Kiley said crisply, "Gone bush, overseas, anywhere. You couldn't have squealed. The world would have laughed themselves silly. Can't you imagine the story in the press, George?" The freckled face was mocking. "Nineteen thousand odd was a small price to pay to save your pride, don't you think? And you still can't squeal," he finished softly.

He bent to look at the mirrored white fluffs of clouds in the water. "I'll have to bring Irene to life again, won't I?" His smile was almost mischievious. "It's got quite out of hand—the whole thing. I didn't count on this. And now you know, so . . . I'll turn her up at Alice perhaps, with a tale of camping in the Territory and never seeing a paper. Will that do?"

"You could have done that long ago. Instead you left us to sweat it out—do you realize," there was no anger, only tiredness in him, "what you've done to Annie and me these past weeks?"

Kiley shrugged. "I thought it would blow over. I didn't want you to know the truth if I could avoid it. Listen, you want to know about the body? I had luck there, George. There was a housing exhibition I covered for the paper—the house was complete right down to a vinyl plastic husband and wife. One of them—life-size, George, soft and pliant and quite life-like, went walkabout. No one knew I had it. With a few weights it made an ideal body for you to help me lug out to sea and I added two pounds of steak for ... aroma, shall we say?" He was smiling again.

"You knew I wouldn't ask to see her—to prove ..."

The cruel smile he remembered so well touched the mouth as Kiley said, "Actually Miriam wouldn't have got herself involved in that accident, only she lost her head. Listen, I told you, didn't I, she gets hysterical. That was true. She lost her head and finished up making a statement, but we didn't expect anything to happen. The old chap seemed all right. We didn't know he'd suddenly turn up his toes that way."

Then he turned, his pale eyes raking the other man's face. He said crisply, "All right, George, you've been clever and now you know. Irene will come to life again and the whole thing will blow over."

"There'll still be the fact. I disposed of her cat, left a note on her door, had her luggage—and lied about the lot," George reminded.

Kiley shrugged, "The police can't touch you. She'll be alive and kicking and she'll give her evidence if it's needed about that accident and that'll be that. You've no choice, George. It's that or the truth coming out. And I'm not paying the cash back. Put it down to experience, George. Expensive, but you'll look twice at a story next time, won't you?"

There was no embarrassment about him, only a calm confidence that he was still safe.

Even when George said flatly, "It's no good, Kiley. The whole story's coming out. I'm not living under suspicion and gossip and malice any longer," Kiley only looked incredulous.

"Isn't that better than being a laughing stock? Think of it, George—the whole story of how you were the biggest fool in the country. The big mogul, they call you that, don't they, duped like a country bumpkin—can't you hear the laughter?"

"I've told the police," George said quietly. "I've told them already."

Kiley's voice stopped. He said, "You've told ... they wouldn't believe you! No one would believe you! No ..."

"I think they do. They came with me anyway. And they're waiting for you. It's up to them now and the courts. And I think they'll believe me, Kiley—no matter how they laugh afterwards."

He saw the pale gaze go beyond him, then behind the pool. He saw Kiley start to move away and saw the men that came forward, beginning to hurry. Then Kiley stopped. He stood facing the police and waited. He was even slightly smiling, as though even then he was confident of carrying it off.

But George was moving too. He didn't look back. He went hurrying across the grass and the pigeons scattered and whirled about him. He didn't see them, or hear their cries. He was intent only on the woman with flame-red hair who awaited his coming.

ABOUT THE AUTHOR

Patricia Carlon was born in Wagga Wagga in 1927. She was educated at various schools in New South Wales before settling in Sydney. She continues to write, is a prize-winning cook, a keen gardener and lives surrounded by her cats.

She has written everything from articles, short stories and serials to short and long novels. Her work has been published in Australia and England under various names in daily papers, magazines and on radio. Much of her pseudonymous writing has been romantic fiction. Her most substantial work, however, encompasses crime and thriller novels, of which she has published at least fourteen. These were first published between 1961 and 1970 in England, mostly by Hodder and Stoughton in the King Crime series. Many have also been published in other European countries and her work has been translated into seven languages.

She was awarded Commonwealth Literary Fellowships in 1970 and 1973.

Her crime novels were not published in Australia, rejected in the sixties because publishers there, in her words, "didn't want anything but police procedure stuff."

SOHO CRIME
Other Titles in this Series

JANWILLEM VAN DE WETERING